It had been a very long time since Meredith West had been so intensely aware of a man.

She held no illusions about her desirability as a woman. She'd always been a bodyguard first, a woman second, more in touch with her abilities to exist in a man's world than in her feminine one.

She got up from the table. Now that Chase had done what she'd wanted him to do in looking through the files, she felt the need to escape. The kitchen felt too small, his presence too big.

He rose and moved to stand within inches of her. His clean, masculine scent once again infused her head, making her half-dizzy.

She stared at him, wondering if she'd ever breathe normally again. Meredith had spent most of her life wishing she were a boy—but at this moment she was intensely grateful that she was a woman.

Dear Reader,

I have been blessed in my life to enjoy the love and companionship of my mother. While writing *Safety in Numbers,* I explored the holes a woman might have inside her in being raised without a mother's love and support. Meredith West never knew her mother, who died when Meredith was little, but she feels her mother's love in her heart and in her soul.

I share so many things with my mom, my thoughts, my emotions and laughter...especially laughter. She will be with me for the rest of my life, in my heart, in my soul.

So here's to mothers everywhere...and to the daughters who love them.

Carla

CARLA CASSIDY

Safety In Numbers

Silhouette®
Romantic
SUSPENSE

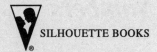 **SILHOUETTE BOOKS**

ISBN-13: 978-0-373-27533-5
ISBN-10:   0-373-27533-1

SAFETY IN NUMBERS

CARLA CASSIDY

is an award-winning author who has written over fifty novels for Silhouette Books. In 1995, she won Best Silhouette Romance for *Anything for Danny*, and in 1998, she also won a Career Achievement Award for Best Innovative Series, both awarded by *Romantic Times BOOKreviews*.

To Rhonda, my other daughter who drives me crazy!

Prologue

He stood beneath the awning of Marsh's Hardware Store and watched the tall, dark-haired woman as she crossed the street. A rush of adrenaline filled him as he noted the long-legged, loose-hipped walk more appropriate for a runway in Paris than for crossing a dusty street in Cotter Creek, Oklahoma.

She looked more like her mother every day. He closed his eyes for a moment, remembering the beautiful Elizabeth West. She'd been like nothing this little nowhere town had ever seen. She'd bewitched him, haunted his days and nights until he knew if he didn't have her he'd go insane.

Narrowing his gaze he watched Elizabeth's daughter until she disappeared through the café doors. He drew a deep, shallow breath, fighting the surge of adrenaline that coursed through him.

It was as if fate was giving him a second chance. If he could possess Elizabeth's daughter it would be almost like having Elizabeth. The thought sent a shiver of sweet anticipation through him.

Yes, fate was giving him another chance, and this time he wouldn't screw it up. It had ended badly with Elizabeth. He'd lost his temper and she'd wound up dead.

He'd do things differently this time. He'd get her to want him and he'd try, he'd really, really try not to lose his temper.

Chapter 1

She felt it again, that creepy-crawly feeling at the nape of her neck, like somebody was staring at her. Meredith West sat up straighter in the booth and glanced around the café as a chill walked up her spine.

It was the usual lunch crowd, locals seated at booths and tables sharing conversation along with the Sunny Side Up Café fare. Nobody suspicious lurked in the corners to give her the odd feeling.

"What's wrong?" Savannah Clarion asked.

Meredith flushed, feeling ridiculous but unable to dismiss the sense of unease that had struck her at odd times of the day and night for the past couple of weeks. "Nothing," she replied. "I guess I've just been a little on edge lately." There was no way she could explain to anyone the feeling she had of impending doom, of her life exploding out of control.

"Gee, I wonder why?" Savannah smiled wryly, the gesture causing her freckles to dance impishly across her nose. "It wouldn't have anything to do with the fact that we've just uncovered a huge ugly conspiracy right here in Cotter Creek, would it?"

As usual, Savannah didn't wait for a reply, but continued, "Everyone is more than a little on edge lately. I can't wait until those FBI agents wipe these dusty streets with the bad guys' behinds."

Meredith laughed and smiled at the red-haired woman across from her. How nice it was that her brother Joshua had fallen in love with Savannah, who was Meredith's best friend.

The strange sensation that had momentarily gripped Meredith eased somewhat. She picked up a fry and dragged it through a pool of ketchup, then popped it into her mouth and chewed thoughtfully.

Maybe it was all the craziness in the town that had her feeling so off center. It had only been a couple of weeks since Savannah had almost been killed after discovering that somebody was working with a corporation to buy up as much of Cotter Creek, Oklahoma, land as possible.

The MoTwin Corporation had conspired to obtain the land to create a community of luxury condominiums and town houses. With the help of Joshua, Savannah had uncovered a plot that involved the murders of half a dozen local ranchers.

The investigation was being taken out of the hands of local law enforcement and the FBI was now conducting the case.

Meredith frowned. "I can't believe they only sent two agents."

Savannah shrugged. "I don't care how many there are as long as they get the job done."

Meredith smiled. "Have you seen them yet? They're sure not going for subtlety with their suits and ties. They look as much out of place as a palm tree would look growing out of our stables."

Savannah leaned back in the booth and eyed Meredith. "I see you've been cutting your hair again."

Meredith raised a hand to her bangs and touched them self-consciously. "I just did a little trim."

Savannah laughed. "What did you use? A buzz saw?"

"There are times I don't find you half as amusing as you find yourself."

Savannah laughed again, then sobered. "I don't know why you don't take time to go to the Curl Palace and get one of the ladies to give you a real haircut and style."

Meredith stabbed another fry into her ketchup. "And why would I do that? I've got no reason to fancy myself up."

"If you'd fancy yourself up just a little you'd have all the single men in Cotter Creek vying for your attention."

"Half the men in town grew up thinking of me

as a little sister, the other half were scared to death of my brothers. I don't want their attention. Just because you're madly in love with Joshua doesn't mean it's your job to see that I find a man. All I need right now is work."

"Joshua has been complaining about how slow things are at Wild West Protective Services right now," Savannah said.

Meredith nodded. "Things have definitely been slow. It's been over a month since I've had an assignment."

Wild West Protective Services was the family-owned business that provided bodyguard and protection services around the country. Meredith worked for the business along with her five brothers.

"I'm not used to so much downtime. It makes me nervous," she said.

And maybe that was what was causing her feeling of unease, she thought. Too much downtime. Or perhaps her disquiet was because of the dreams she'd been having lately, dreams of her dead mother.

She glanced around the café once again, then focused back on Savannah. "I'm thinking about asking Sheriff Ramsey to reopen the investigation into my mother's murder," she said.

Savannah stared at her in surprise. "Talk about a cold case. It's been what…twenty years?"

"Twenty-five. I was three years old when she was murdered." Meredith shoved her plate aside, her appetite gone. "I've been having dreams about her." She frowned thoughtfully. "It's like she can't rest in peace until I find out who killed her."

"After all this time I'd think the odds were pretty poor that you'd discover who was responsible." Savannah eyed her friend worriedly. "You're right, you have too much time on your hands at the moment."

Meredith flashed a quick smile. "Maybe, but I am going to talk about it with Sheriff Ramsey."

Savannah's gaze shot over Meredith's shoulder. "You won't believe the hunk that just walked in the front door."

"Does Joshua know you talk about other men like that?"

Savannah raised a copper-colored eyebrow. "Honey, I love your brother, but I know a hunk when I see one." Her eyes widened. "And this one is coming our way."

The words were barely out of her mouth before he appeared at the side of their booth. In her first glance, Meredith registered several things. He was a tall drink of water, topped by sandy-colored hair, with ice-blue eyes that pierced rather than gazed.

Even though he was blond and blue-eyed there was nothing of a pretty boy about him. His face was lean, all angles that combined to give him a slightly dangerous aura. A faint white scar bisected one of his eyebrows. His presence seemed to fill the room with a pulsating energy.

"Meredith West?"

She jumped in surprise at his deep, smooth voice. "Yes? I'm Meredith."

"My name is Chase McCall. I'm a friend of your brother Dalton. He sent me over here to find you and ask if you'd be kind enough to take my mother and me to the ranch. This is my mother, Kathy."

It was only then that Meredith realized he wasn't alone. Next to him stood a short, white-haired woman with blue eyes and a sweet smile. "Hello, dear. It's a pleasure to meet you," she said. Despite the snowy hair on her head, there was a youthful sparkle in her eyes.

Meredith vaguely remembered Dalton mentioning something about friends coming to town, but at the time he'd mentioned it she hadn't paid much attention.

"And I'm Savannah Clarion," Savannah said. "Is it business or pleasure that brings you to Cotter Creek?"

Meredith wasn't surprised by Savannah's question. As Cotter Creek's star newspaper reporter, she had a healthy curiosity about everyone.

"Strictly pleasure," Kathy McCall replied, her eyes twinkling with good humor. "We decided to take a little trip together, you know mother/son bonding time, and Chase had heard so many things from Dalton about the charming Cotter Creek. So, here we are."

A flash of impatience shot across Chase's features. "We've had a long bus ride to get here and we'd really like to get settled in."

"You came by bus?" Meredith looked at him in surprise. Neither of them had any luggage.

"Somebody thought it would be a great idea," he said tersely.

Kathy's smile made her look like a good-humored cherub. "It was lovely to see the scenery without worrying about Chase getting a speeding ticket or two."

"Where's your luggage?" Meredith asked. She'd been in the bodyguard business too long to simply trust the word of two strangers who had appeared at her booth in the local café.

"We left it over at the office with Dalton," Chase replied.

Meredith stood and grabbed her coat and purse from the booth. As she did she couldn't help but notice that Chase's gaze swept the length of her, then he glanced away, as if dismissing her as not worthy of his attention.

She'd known the man less than three minutes and already something about him made her want to grind her teeth. She fumbled with her wallet for money to pay her lunch tab.

"Don't worry about it," Savannah said. "I'll get it this time. You can get it next time."

Meredith flashed her friend a grateful smile, then straightened and looked at Chase.

"Shall we?"

As she exited the café she was acutely conscious of the man following her. Handsome men weren't anything new to Meredith. She'd been raised with five brothers who most women considered unusually attractive. But in that first instance of laying eyes on Chase McCall, uncharacteristic butterflies had flitted erratically in her stomach. Meredith wasn't used to butterflies.

Kathy fell into step beside her as they walked toward the Wild West Protective Services office just down the street. "We thought we'd be staying with Dalton, but he said we'd be much more comfortable at the ranch," she said.

Meredith thought of her brother's one-bedroom apartment in town. "Dalton's place is pretty small and not real welcoming to guests. The ranch is much better," she agreed, although she wasn't at all sure she liked the idea of sharing her home space with the tall, silent man who walked just behind them. "We're used to company at the ranch."

As they entered the Wild West Protective Services office, Dalton stood from the desk. "Ah good, I see you found her," he said to Chase.

"Your description made it easy," Chase replied, a whisper of amusement evident in his voice.

Meredith turned to look at her brother. "And just what kind of description did you tell him?"

Dalton's cheeks reddened slightly as a sheepish grin stole over his lips. "It doesn't matter now," Chase replied smoothly. "We found you and that's all that's important." He picked up the two suitcases by the door and looked at her expectantly. For somebody who was on vacation he didn't look particularly eager to have a good time.

"Unfortunately I'm expecting a phone call that I need to take, otherwise I'd drive you to the ranch myself. But Meredith will get you settled in, then I'll see you this evening at dinnertime." Dalton smiled at her. "Take good care of them, sis."

She smiled at Dalton, but as her gaze fell on Chase McCall, the strange feeling of disquiet swept through her once again, making her uncomfortable and, oddly, just a little bit afraid.

Chase McCall sat in the back seat of the four-door sedan, leaving the two women in the front to chat. As Meredith drove she talked to Kathy about the town and the unusual cold snap of weather and the family ranch.

"You're here just in time for the Fall Festival," she said. "There's a parade on Saturday afternoon, then a big dance Saturday night."

He stared out the window at the passing scenery, wishing he were anywhere else. He couldn't think of anyone who needed a vacation more than he did, but this wasn't a vacation and he was here under false pretenses.

He glanced up and in the rearview mirror he caught Meredith West gazing at him. As he met her gaze, she quickly looked away and he looked back out the side window.

She'd been a surprise. Dalton had talked a little about his sister. In the days that Dalton and Chase had spent together, Dalton had talked about all of his family. He'd told Chase that his sister was tough, committed to her work as a bodyguard and preferred the company of her horse to most people.

But there was a wealth of things he hadn't mentioned about Meredith. Dalton hadn't told him she had eyes the color of an early-summer lawn or that her legs were long and lean beneath her tight jeans. He hadn't mentioned that her hair was dark mahogany or that her skin was flawless.

In that first moment of seeing her, a quick electric shock had sizzled through him; a shock of physical attraction he hadn't felt for a very long time.

It reminded him just how long it had been since he'd held a woman in his arms, felt sweet satisfied sighs against the crook of his neck.

He suddenly realized the women had gone silent and Kathy had turned her head to look at him expectantly. "Did I miss something?" he asked.

Kathy looked at Meredith and smiled. "You'll have to excuse my son. He sometimes forgets his social skills. Meredith asked you what you did for a living, dear."

Again those green eyes flashed in the mirror. Not warm and welcoming, but rather cool and wary. "I'm a Kansas City cop." It was the first of many lies he'd probably tell over the next couple of days.

"And is that where you met my brother? In Kansas City?" she asked. The eyes disappeared from the mirror once again.

"Yeah, he was working the Milton case last year

and we coordinated with him. Dalton and I struck up a friendship. We've stayed in touch through e-mail since then."

"When Chase decided to take his vacation time and mentioned he was coming out here, I just insisted he bring me along," Kathy said. "He stays so busy we rarely have quality time together."

"Our place is just ahead," Meredith said as she turned off the road and down a lane. Chase once again looked out the window with interest. He knew the West family was one of the largest landowners in the county.

He'd researched their entire clan before taking the assignment. Red West, the patriarch, had come from California to Cotter Creek as a young man and had begun his business, Wild West Protective Services. The business had grown along with his family.

He and his wife had six children before Elizabeth West was murdered. Since her death, Red had worked to establish Wild West Protective Services as one of the most reputable bodyguard agencies in the country.

On the surface the family looked for the most part like the American dream. But a couple of anonymous tips phoned into the FBI office said otherwise. His job was to dig beneath the surface and find any darkness that might be hidden, a darkness that might have led somebody in the West family to sell out an entire town.

"Here we are," Meredith said as she pulled to a

halt in front of a large, sprawling ranch house. It was impressive, the big house with its wraparound porch. As far as the eye could see were outbuildings and pastureland.

As they got out of the car and Chase got the suitcases out of the trunk, a tall man appeared on the front porch, a smile of welcome on his face. By the time they reached the porch another man had joined him. The short, gray-haired man had blue eyes that held a touch of wariness. "Welcome," the tall man said and held out a hand to Chase. "I'm Red West."

Introductions were made all the way around. The short older man was introduced as Smokey Johnson, head cook and bottle washer for the clan.

As Chase followed him through the front door, he had a feeling that Smokey Johnson was a man who might not be easily fooled. He and Kathy would have to be careful around the old man. But Chase didn't expect any of the West family to be fooled easily.

"Oh my, this is just lovely," Kathy exclaimed as they entered the living room. "I hope we aren't putting you out."

"Nonsense, nothing we like better than company," Red assured her. "Meredith, why don't we get them settled in their rooms, then we'll have Smokey rustle up some refreshments. It's a long bus ride from Kansas City to here."

"That sounds wonderful," Kathy said.

"We'll put Kathy in the guest room and Chase can go into Tanner's old room," Red said.

For the first time since they'd stepped into the house, Chase focused on Meredith. She had the face of a beauty queen, but if her hair were any indication of the local stylist's expertise then he wouldn't be visiting any of the town's barbers. Although a luxurious black, her bangs fell unevenly across her forehead and the left side of the shoulder-length locks was definitely shorter than the right side.

There wasn't an ounce of makeup on her face, that he could see, and she was dressed in a pair of jeans and an oversize man's flannel shirt. Once again a small ball of unexpected tension twisted in his gut.

Her gaze met his and her cheeks pinkened slightly. "If you'll follow me, I'll show you to your rooms," she said.

She led Kathy to a room decorated in cheerful yellow with an adjoining bath. Chase set Kathy's suitcase on the bed, then followed Meredith down the hall. Even though the flannel shirt struck her below the hips, it didn't hide the sensual sway of her walk.

The bedroom she led him to was smaller than Kathy's and had obviously been occupied by a male. The bed was a heavy mahogany covered in a navy spread. A chest of drawers stood against one wall. "Tanner? Which one is that?" he asked as he set his suitcase down.

"Tanner is my oldest brother," she said.

"The one who married a princess."

"That's right. Anna." Her chin rose a touch and she met his gaze. "Tell me, what description did my brother give of me that made me so easy to find in the café?"

"He said to look for the gorgeous, sexy woman who looked like she'd had a close encounter with a Weed Eater." He gazed pointedly at her uneven hair.

She raised a hand self-consciously, but before she touched her hair, she dropped her arm and narrowed her eyes, obviously not pleased as she edged toward the door.

"The bathroom is just down the hall on the left. Feel free to head to the kitchen after you get settled in." She slid out of the room as if she couldn't escape him fast enough.

He pulled his suitcase onto the bed and opened it. He'd improvised a bit on what Dalton had said. Dalton had called his sister neither gorgeous nor sexy.

As he hung some of his clothing in the closet, he wondered how difficult it had been for Meredith West to be raised in a house filled with men. By the look of her she certainly didn't seem to be in touch with her femininity. Not that it mattered to him. Not that he cared.

He wasn't here to care about anyone. He was here to do a job. It was bad enough he was here to betray a friend's trust; the only thing that could make it worse was if he also seduced his friend's sister.

Chapter 2

There was no way Dalton would have described her as gorgeous or sexy, although he certainly would have told Chase she looked like a woman who'd gotten too close to a Weed Eater.

Meredith thought about that all through dinner that night. Dalton had arrived at the ranch to share the meal and visit with his friends. Meredith had eaten quickly, then excused herself and retreated to the stables until bedtime.

Now, the faint gray of predawn painted the sky as she crept from her bedroom and down the hallway to the bathroom. As she showered and dressed for the day, her thoughts lingered on Chase McCall.

Gorgeous and sexy. He had to say that. Had he

been making fun of her? Nobody had ever used those terms to describe her.

She didn't like him and she wasn't sure why. He'd been pleasant enough at dinner the night before, entertaining them with cop stories and talking about the good times he and Dalton had shared while they'd worked on the same case.

But there was an edge to him, a whisper of something slightly dangerous in his eyes, an arrogant tilt to his head. She stood in front of the mirror and brushed her shoulder-length hair, then frowned.

Maybe Savannah was right. She needed to get into the Curl Palace and get one of the ladies to trim her hair the right way.

Fighting her impulse to pick up a pair of scissors and try to straighten out the mess, she reached for her toothbrush instead. She always cut her hair when she was stressed, and there was no denying that she'd been stressed lately.

She'd go to the Curl Palace this morning, then head over to Sheriff Ramsey's office to see if she could get her hands on the files of the investigation into her mother's murder.

She had a feeling Ramsey wouldn't be particularly pleased by her request. "As if we don't have enough going on around here," she could imagine him saying.

She finished brushing her teeth, then gave her hair a final finger comb. Her decision to get her hair professionally cut and styled had absolutely nothing to do with Chase McCall, she told herself. She would have done it whether the handsome man had come to town or not.

Leaving the bathroom, she was glad that Tanner's bedroom door remained closed. It was early enough that she didn't expect anyone to be up except Smokey, who would be in the kitchen working on breakfast.

Instead of heading into the kitchen, she walked to the front door and slipped outside to the porch. She moved directly to the railing and leaned against it, staring out at the land that stretched for miles all around.

This was her favorite time of day, when the sun was just starting to peek over the horizon and birds sang from the trees. Scents of hay and grass and cattle wafted on the air, as familiar to her as her own reflection in a mirror.

She loved the ranch, but there were times when she longed for the excitement of the city, the anonymity of a place where she wasn't one of those West kids, but rather simply Meredith West.

She drew deep breaths, filling herself up with the smells of home, then turned to go back inside. She jumped, startled as she saw the old man seated in the wicker rocking chair.

"Smokey! Jeez, you scared me half to death. What are you doing out here?" Even in the dim light she could see the frown that tugged his grizzled eyebrows together in an uneven unibrow.

"That woman is in my kitchen."

"Kathy? What's she doing?"

"Cooking." The word spat from him as if he found it distasteful on his tongue.

A small burst of laughter welled up inside Meredith, but she quickly swallowed it. As far as Smokey was concerned invasion of his kitchen was grounds for execution. "Think I'll go get a cup of coffee and check things out," she said.

Smokey merely grunted in response.

Meredith found the attractive white-haired woman in the kitchen cutting up fruit. "Ah, another early riser," she said in greeting to Meredith.

"You're supposed to be on vacation," Meredith said as she poured herself a cup of coffee, then perched at the island where Kathy worked.

"There's nothing I love more than cooking, especially for other people, but I rarely get a chance." She smiled at Meredith. "I told Smokey that I'd take over this morning and give him a little vacation. Besides, I'm not sure he was feeling well this morning. He looked positively gray when he left the kitchen."

"He's just not used to somebody else taking over his duties," Meredith replied.

Kathy smiled once again, a hint of steel in her baby blues. "Well, he'll just have to get used to it. I intend to pull my own weight around here and at my age about the only thing I am good for is cooking."

It was going to be an interesting couple of days, Meredith mused. At that moment Chase entered the kitchen clad in a pair of jeans and a navy knit shirt that clung to his broad shoulders and flat stomach. The sight of him filled her with an inexplicable tension.

"Good morning," he said as he walked to the countertop where the coffeemaker sat.

"'Morning," Meredith replied. "I hope you slept well."

"I always do." He carried his cup and sat on the stool next to Meredith, bringing with him the faint scent of shaving cream, minty soap and a woodsy cologne. The tension inside her coiled a little tighter. "What about you? How did you sleep?"

It was a simple question, but something about the look in his eyes made her feel like he was prying into intimate territory. "I always sleep well, too," she replied.

He took a sip of his coffee, then looked at her curiously. "Dalton mentioned last night that we've come to town at a time when things are pretty unsettled," he said.

"Very unsettled," she agreed, relaxing a bit as the subject changed.

"Tell me about it."

"It's complicated, but a couple of weeks ago we discovered that a corporation called MoTwin has been buying up property in the area."

"That doesn't sound unusual. Corporations seem to be buying up property everywhere in the United States," Kathy observed.

"Yes, but in this case, the land they were buying

was from ranchers who had died, ranchers who had been murdered."

"Oh, my," Kathy exclaimed, then picked up her knife to continue cutting up a kiwi.

"The deaths were made to look like accidents, so it took a while for anyone to realize what was going on," Meredith continued. "The latest death was a real estate agent who had written up the property contracts on the land in question. She was murdered. A couple of FBI agents are here now working the case. We know somebody in town has to be behind the scheme, somebody local has orchestrated the deaths and that's who we want."

"This MoTwin, what do you know about it?" Chase asked.

"Not much." Meredith took a sip of her coffee, then continued, "The address on all the paperwork is nothing more than an empty storefront location in Boston. Two men are listed as partners, Joe Black and Harold Willington, but as far as I know nobody has been able to find them or dig up any information on them. We know that the land was apparently being bought up for a community of luxury condos and town houses."

She took another sip of her coffee and fought off a chill at the thought that it could be a friend or a neighbor who was responsible for the deaths in the area.

"Hopefully the FBI will find out who here in town is responsible and they'll lock them up and throw away the key," she exclaimed. "In any case, it shouldn't interfere with your visit here. By the way, how long are you intending on staying?"

Chase's gaze was lazy and his blue eyes sparked with humor. "Trying to get rid of us already?"

"Of course not," she replied hurriedly. "I was just curious." Curious as to how long she'd have to put up with the strange feeling he evoked inside her.

"We aren't sure," Chase replied. "I have quite a bit of vacation time built up so we're kind of open-ended at the moment."

Kathy glanced at the clock on the wall. "I'd better get back to work if I'm going to have breakfast ready at a reasonable time. Why don't you two shoo and let me do my thing."

Meredith drained her coffee cup, placed it in the dishwasher, then started out of the kitchen. "Where are you headed?" Chase asked.

"To the stables," she replied. "I usually go out there every morning and most evenings to say hello to the horses."

"Mind if I tag along?"

Yes, I do. You make me nervous and I don't know why. She didn't say that, but instead shook her head. She grabbed a jacket from a hook next to the back door, and once she stepped off the porch, Chase fell in beside her.

"Dalton told me you're quite a horseback rider," he said as they crossed the thick, browning lawn toward the stables.

At five-ten there were few men who dwarfed Meredith, but Chase did. He made her feel small and oddly vulnerable. "Do you ride?" she asked.

"Motorcycles, not horses."

"Then you don't know what you're missing," she replied, her steps long and brisk. They walked for a few minutes in silence.

"Quite a spread you have here," he said. "Did this MoTwin Corporation contact you all about selling out? You said the deaths that occurred were made to look like accidents. Anything odd happen to your father?"

She stopped in her tracks and turned to face him with narrowed eyes. "For somebody just visiting the area you have a lot of questions."

"I'm a cop. Curiosity comes natural to me."

She gazed at him for a long moment, taking in the handsome chiseled features, the spark of the early-morning sun on his hair and the guileless blue of his eyes. "Then to answer your question, no. Nobody has contacted my father about selling because they probably know that won't ever happen. And no, nothing strange or suspicious has happened to my father.

"One thing all those dead ranchers had in common was either no children or family to take over their ranches, or kin that weren't interested in ranching. My father has five sons and me. Killing him wouldn't get anyone any closer to owning this place."

He frowned thoughtfully. "But, I would think if

this corporation planned a community of condos and town houses, they'd want this land." He cast a gaze around. "It looks pretty prime to me."

"I don't know what the intentions of MoTwin were where our land was concerned. I can't begin to guess what was in those men's heads."

They reached the stables and walked inside, where the horses in the various stalls greeted their presence with snickers and soft whinnies.

As she walked toward where her horse, Spooky, was stalled, she paused at each of the other stalls to pet a nose or scratch an ear. She tried to ignore Chase's nearness, but it was darned near impossible.

The man seemed to fill the stable interior with an unsettling presence that even the horses felt. They sidestepped and pawed the ground with an unusual restlessness, as if catching the scent of a predator in the air.

"Tell me about your other brothers," he said as she greeted her black mare with a soft whisper. "Your father mentioned they'd all be here for dinner tonight. I'd like to know a little about them before then. Dalton has mentioned them in the past, but never went into specific details."

"Tanner's the oldest. He's thirty-five and as you know married to Anna. Zack is thirty-one and married to Kate. He's running for Sheriff. Clay is thirty and just married Libby, who also has a little girl named Gracie. Then there's Joshua. He's the baby at twenty-five and he's dating my best friend, Savannah. You met her yes-terday at the café."

He nodded, his eyes dark and enigmatic. "Do you all still work for the family business?"

"We did, but things are changing. Tanner was actively running things before he met and married Anna. They're now building a house and he's involved in that and not working so much right now. As I mentioned, Zack wants to be sheriff and it looks like he's going to get his wish. The man who's working as sheriff right now has plans to retire."

She scratched Spooky behind the ears, finding it much easier to focus on the horse's loving, brown eyes than Chase's cold blue ones.

"Joshua still works for the business and so do I, but for the last couple of months things have been rather slow." She gave the horse a final pat on the neck. "We should probably head back to the house for breakfast."

"So, what do you do in your spare time?" he asked as they made their way to the house.

"I occasionally do some volunteer work, but most of the time I keep busy around here. Running a ranch the size of ours requires lots of work."

"Dalton mentioned to me last night that you don't date. Why not?"

She stopped walking and held his gaze. "First of all, my brothers don't know everything that goes on in my life. Just because they don't know what I'm doing doesn't mean I'm not doing it. And secondly, it's really none of your business."

She didn't wait for his reply, but instead hurried toward the house, needing some space from the man, his endless questions and the hot lick of desire just looking at him stirred inside her.

It was just after ten when Chase sat in the passenger seat of Meredith's car. She'd mentioned at breakfast that she was heading into town to run some errands and he'd asked if he could hitch a ride with her. He could tell the idea didn't thrill her, but she was too polite to tell him no.

He'd told her that while she ran her errands or whatever, he'd hang out at the Wild West Protective Services office with Dalton.

He'd known most of the information she'd told him in the stables before he'd even asked the questions, but he'd hoped she'd give him something that would either exonerate or condemn somebody guilty.

The Wests might never have made the FBI radar if it hadn't been for a couple of anonymous tips that had come in pointing a finger at the family. He had no idea if the tips were valid or not. It was his and Kathy's assignment to find out.

"You asked me about my family earlier," she said, breaking the uncomfortable silence that had existed between them since they'd gotten into the car. "Tell me about yours."

As always, when Chase thought of what little family he'd had, a knot of tension twisted in his chest.

He reached up and touched the slightly raised scar that slashed through his eyebrow, then dropped his hand.

"There's not much to tell. It's just my mother and me. My father died a couple of years ago. He was a miserable man who gambled away his money, then drank and got mean."

It was a partial truth. His mother had died when he was five and his violent, drunken father had raised him until Chase turned sixteen and left home. Whenever Chase thought of his family he got a sick feeling in the pit of his stomach. God save him from people who professed to love him.

"I'm sorry," she said. "But your mother seems very nice."

He grinned. "Kat…Mom is a jewel. She left my father when I was ten and we have a great relationship." This was the cover story they'd concocted, a blend of half lies and half truths. Kathy was a jewel, not as a mother but as a partner.

"She stepped into dangerous territory this morning."

Chase looked at her curiously. "What do you mean?"

"She took over Smokey's kitchen."

"That's bad?"

She smiled and in the genuine warmth of the gesture she was so stunning that the blood in Chase's veins heated. "That's grounds for a firing squad. Smokey has always been fiercely territorial about his kitchen."

"What's his story? He's not part of the family, right?" Although Chase had no idea what financial benefit Smokey Johnson might get from conspiring with MoTwin, he knew that not all motives revolved around money.

"He's family. He might as well have been born a West," Meredith replied. "He worked as the ranch manager for years, then took a nasty spill from a horse and crushed his leg. He was still healing from that when my mother was murdered."

"That must have been tough on everyone." He watched the play of emotions that crossed her features, a flash of pain, a twist of anger, then finally the smooth transition into a weary acceptance. She'd be an easy mark at cards. She didn't have much of a poker face.

"From what I understand, my father was devastated. He and my mother had one of those loves that you only read about in novels. They were best friends and soul mates and Dad crawled deep into his grief. Smokey stepped in to help with all of us kids and he never left. He's a combination of a drill sergeant and a beloved uncle."

She pulled into a parking space in front of the Wild West Protective Services office. She shut off the car engine and unbuckled her seat belt. "Why don't I meet you back here around noon and we'll head back to the ranch."

"Why don't we meet back here at noon and I'll buy us lunch at the café?"

She looked at him in surprise. "Why would you want to do that?"

"Why wouldn't I?" he countered. "It's not every day I get the opportunity to buy lunch for a pretty lady." He watched her, fascinated by the pink blush that swept into her cheeks.

"I guess it would be all right to have lunch before we head back," she replied.

They got out of her car and she murmured goodbye, then headed across the street. "What are you doing, Chase," he muttered to himself as he watched her walk away.

Once again, she was dressed in an old flannel shirt and a pair of worn jeans. She intrigued him. She acted and dressed like a woman who didn't much care about a man's attention, and yet the blush that had colored her cheeks had spoken otherwise.

She was unlike any woman he'd ever been around before. Most of the women he dated were girly girls, high-maintenance savvy singles who cared even less about a committed relationship than he did. Meredith West blushed like a woman who wasn't accustomed to compliments or attention.

He watched until she disappeared into a store-front, then he turned and went into the Wild West Protective Services office.

"I don't care how difficult the client is," Dalton said into the phone receiver as he raised a hand in greeting to Chase. "You do what you have to do to make this right. You know how to do your job, just do it and try not to make people angry." He hung up the phone with a groan. "I think sometimes it's easier to have a boss than to be one."

Chase sat in one of the chairs in front of the desk and grinned at his friend. "As one who has a boss instead of being one, I'd argue the fact with you."

Dalton laughed and leaned forward in his chair. "How about one night you and I make plans to shoot some pool and drink a few beers?"

"Sounds good to me," Chase agreed. Maybe knocking back a few brews would get thoughts of Meredith West out of his head.

The two men visited for a few minutes, then Dalton got another phone call and Chase left the office to wander the sidewalks and see what kind of vibes he picked up.

Being around Dalton was almost as difficult as being with Meredith. The deception of his friend didn't sit well. But Chase had a job to do and work had always been the one thing he could depend on, the only thing he clung to.

Cotter Creek was a pleasant little town with sidewalks and shade trees running the length of Main Street. Benches every twenty feet or so welcomed people to sit a spell.

An old man sat on the bench outside the barbershop, his weatherworn face showing no emotion as Chase sat on the opposite end of the bench.

"Nice day," Chase said.

"Seen better," the old man replied.

"My name's Chase, I'm here in town visiting the West family."

"Too many strangers popping up here in Cotter Creek for my comfort and I'm Sam Rhenquist."

Chase leaned back against the bench. "Nice town."

"Used to be. Lately everybody's been looking cross-eyed at each other, wondering who might be guilty of some things that have happened around here." Rhenquist eyed him with a touch of suspicion and clamped his mouth closed, as if irritated that he'd said too much.

For the next few minutes Chase tried some small talk, but the old man was having nothing to do with it. Finally Chase rose, said goodbye and headed down the sidewalk with no particular destination in mind.

He knew the best place to pick up information would be the café or wherever Dalton intended to take him for the night of beer and pool. People talked when they ate, and people really talked when they drank. No telling what little tidbit he'd be able to pick up that might help the investigation.

Eventually he wanted to touch base with Bill Wallace and Roger Tompkins, the two agents who were actively working the case here in town. He wanted to know who they had in their radar and what they might have discovered in the brief time they'd been in town.

It didn't take him long to walk the length of the businesses on Main Street, then he crossed the street and headed back the way he'd come on the opposite side of the street. As he walked, his mind whirled.

He'd already learned two important things since arriving in town. The first was that Meredith West was sharp and he'd have to be more subtle with his questions than he'd been when they'd gone to the stables that morning.

The second was that for some crazy reason he was intensely attracted to the tall, dark-haired woman. If he allowed that attraction to get out of hand, he'd risk complicating his job here.

He'd share a simple lunch with her, then head out to the ranch and hope that Kathy had managed to glean some sort of helpful information about the rest of the West family.

He made it back to Meredith's car and leaned against the driver's side to wait for Meredith to return from whatever she was doing. It was damned inconvenient not to have a car at his disposal.

It had been Kathy's idea to ride the bus into town. She'd thought being at the mercy of the West family for transportation would afford them more time to chat with the various members of the clan.

He should have put his foot down and told her it was a dumb idea, but he found it difficult to argue with Kathy about anything. Those twinkling blue eyes and sweet smile of hers hid a stubborn streak that always surprised him.

He straightened as he saw Meredith in the distance coming toward him. As she drew closer, he realized she looked different…softer…more feminine. It took him a minute to realize it was her hair.

Where before it had hung without rhyme, without reason in various lengths, it now feathered around her face, emphasizing the classic beauty of her features. She carried with her a large file folder bound with several rubber bands.

"Wow," he said when she was close enough to hear him.

Her cheeks reddened slightly and she reached up to self-consciously touch a strand of her hair. "It's just a haircut," she said with a touch of belligerence.

"No, it's more than that. It's a total transformation," he replied.

"It's not a big deal," she replied, obviously not wanting him to make it a big deal. "You ready for lunch?"

He nodded. "What have you got there?"

"Just some paperwork I want to read." She opened the car door, set the papers on the seat, then locked the doors and gestured toward the café. "Shall we?"

The Sunny Side Up Café was in full swing serving a surprisingly large lunch crowd. They found an empty booth toward the back and settled in, but not before Meredith was greeted by half a dozen people.

She'd been attractive before, but with the new hairstyle Chase was having trouble keeping his gaze from her. "Is the food good here?" he asked as he opened a menu and forced himself to look at it. But it couldn't hold his attention the way she did.

"Excellent," she replied. She looked ill at ease, her gaze darting around the room then back at her menu.

"Is everything all right?"

Her bright green eyes met his gaze in surprise. "Yes, everything is fine." Once again she made a quick sweep of the room with her gaze.

"So, tell me about your work," Chase said after the waitress had departed with their orders. "It must be fascinating to be a bodyguard."

"It has its moments," she replied, then frowned. "Although lately there haven't been as many moments as I'd like."

"What do you mean?"

She picked up her napkin and placed it in her lap. "Business has been slow. None of us are working as much as we like."

The conversation halted momentarily as the waitress appeared to serve their drinks. "You mentioned that before. What's made things slow down?" Chase asked when they were once again alone.

"Who knows? I've talked about it some with Tanner, my oldest brother, and even he isn't sure what's caused the slow down. I guess people not needing bodyguard services doesn't necessarily translate to lower crime rates in the city. You must stay very busy."

Chase grinned ruefully. "Definitely. In the war on crime, the bad guys still seem to have the upper hand."

Her gaze held his for a long moment. "Speaking of crime, did Dalton tell you that our mother was murdered years ago?"

She had the kind of eyes that could swallow a man whole and make him forget his surroundings. At the moment they radiated a soft vulnerability, a wistful need he immediately wanted to fulfill, no matter what it entailed.

It was he who broke the eye contact, disconcerted by his own reaction. "Yeah, Dalton told me about it."

"Those papers I left in the car are copies of the reports concerning her murder. It was never solved and lately I've been thinking about it, about her a lot."

There was an unspoken question in her gaze as he looked at her once again. "I thought maybe by looking at the files I might see something that was missed in the initial investigation. I'm not telling my father or my brothers that I'm looking into Mom's death. I don't want to upset anyone." She paused a moment, then continued, "How long have you been a homicide cop?"

He suddenly knew what she wanted from him. "You want me to take a look at those files?"

She flashed him a grateful smile. "Would you mind? Maybe you'll see something important, something that I'm not trained to look for."

"Sure, I don't mind." He'd take a look at the files. It was the least he could do.

A few minutes later, the waitress delivered their food and Chase's mind worked to process his thoughts and impressions. And the one thing that kept coming back into his mind was the fact that business was slow at Wild West Protective Services.

Somebody in Cotter Creek had worked with the men at MoTwin to identify the weak in town, the ranchers without family, the men who could easily be killed and their deaths look like accidents. Money had certainly changed hands…a lot of money. Had Meredith or one of her brothers panicked about the financial status of Wild West Protective Services and made a deal with the devil?

Yes, he'd look at the file concerning her mother's murder and hope that in the end he didn't take another family member away from her.

Chapter 3

Dinner was chaotic. It always was when the entire West family broke bread together. Meredith let the conversation swirl around her, grateful that for the moment nobody was focused on her.

She'd had enough attention when each of her brothers had arrived at the ranch. They'd teased her unmercifully about her new haircut until her father had insisted they stop picking on her.

Red West had gazed at her for a long moment, a softness in his eyes. "You look exactly like your mother did when I fell in love with her," he'd said, then hugged her. "She would have been so proud of you."

His words had merely renewed her desire to get to the bottom of the crime that had stolen her mother. She and Chase had agreed to go over the file that evening, after her family had left and her father went to bed.

She cast a surreptitious glance across the table at Chase, who was in the middle of a conversation with Zack. There was no denying the fact that she was attracted to the Kansas City cop.

It had been over a year since Meredith had enjoyed any kind of relationship with a man. At that time she'd been working in Florida and had fallen into a relationship with a local man. It had lasted over two months, until her job in Florida had ended.

Todd Green had been a terrific guy and she'd hoped when it was time for her to return to Oklahoma that he'd beg her not to go, that he'd tell her he couldn't live without her.

But he hadn't. Instead he'd told her he'd had a lot of fun with her, but when he finally decided to settle down for a long-term committed relationship it would be with somebody softer, somebody less capable...a real woman who needed him.

She'd been devastated. Not so much because she'd been head over heels in love with Todd, but rather because his hurtful words had pierced through to a well of doubt and insecurities she'd secretly harbored.

How could she know what it meant to be a real woman when there had been no woman in her life? She'd learned martial arts and self-defense like her brothers. She'd been taught how to shoot a gun and how to assess a situation for danger. But nobody had taught her how to be a *real* woman.

Since Todd there had been nobody else. Until Chase McCall with his piercing blue eyes that for some reason made her feel oddly lacking whenever he gazed at her.

The talk at the table turned to the Fall Festival dance in three days. "The whole town shows up for the dance," Tanner said. "Except Meredith, she always heads home before the band starts to play."

"We've all decided she must have two left feet," Zack added with a teasing grin. His wife, Kate, elbowed him in his side.

Despite the teasing, there was no denying the sense of unity at the table, the fierce loyalty and love they all felt for each other was on display, no matter who the guests of the house might be at the time.

Chase gazed at Meredith from across the table. "Surely this time you'll stay. If fact, I insist you save me a dance or two just to prove to your brothers that you don't have two left feet."

The idea of being held in his arms even for the length of a song caused a stir of warmth to seep through her blood. She wanted to protest, to tell him that she never went to the local dances, but try as she might, the protest refused to rise to her lips and she found herself nodding her assent.

Chase and his mother had only been in town for three days, but each day had increased the annoying tension in Meredith. She'd tried to keep her distance from him, but it was difficult in the confines of the house.

After dinner there was another hour of small talk, then everyone began to leave. "Meredith, will you walk me to my car?" Dalton asked.

She looked at him in surprise. "All right," she replied. Together brother and sister left the house and stepped outside into the chilly night air. Darkness had fallen and the only light was the faint glow of the moon drifting down from the cloudless sky.

"I assume you wanted to talk to me alone?" Meredith said as they crossed the expanse of yard to where Dalton had parked his car.

"I've got a favor to ask you," Dalton replied. "About the dance on Saturday night. Even though you said you'd be there at the dinner table, I thought you might sneak out early. I know dances aren't your thing, but could you hang around and entertain Chase and his mother for me?"

Meredith had already decided to skip the evening festivities despite the fact that she'd said she would save a dance or two for Chase. Her experiences at the occasional town dances had never been pleasant ones.

"Why do I have to babysit your guests?" she asked, a touch of irritation deepening her tone.

Dalton grinned, leaned over and kissed her lightly on the forehead. "Because you're the best sister in the whole world and I have a date with Melanie Brooks for the dance."

She wanted to decline, she *so* didn't want to do

this, and yet Dalton had never asked her for anything. She also knew he'd spent the past month
working up his nerve to ask pretty Melanie out on
a date. "All right. I said I'd go, so I'll go and make
nice to your friend and his mother."

"You're the best."

"That's what you guys always tell me when
you've managed to talk me into doing something I
don't want to do."

Dalton laughed and got into his car. She watched
as he drove down the lane, his headlights eventually
swallowed up by the darkness of the night.

She wrapped her arms around herself and
remained standing in place for a long moment. She
frowned as she thought about the dance and rubbed
her hands along the soft flannel of her shirt.

She didn't even have anything to wear. Her closet
was filled with jeans and shirts, and the only dress
she owned was the bridesmaid dress she'd worn to
Clay and Libby's wedding. It was floor length and
far too fussy for a town dance.

Maybe she'd talk to Libby tomorrow about bor-
rowing a dress for the night. The two women were
about the same size, and Libby had a closet full of
clothes she'd brought with her when she'd moved
from California to make a life with Clay.

A night breeze blew a burst of chilly air through
the nearby trees. Dying leaves swished against one
another and a chill that had nothing to do with the
night air swept up her spine. Once again she felt that

creepy feeling, like somebody was watching her, like she wasn't quite alone in the night.

She told herself she was being foolish, but turned on her heels and hurried back into the house. She went into the kitchen to see if there was anything she could help Smokey with, but Kathy stood at the sink next to him chatting as she dried the dishes he washed. Smokey wore a long-suffering expression, as if her chatter was about to drive him insane.

Meredith's father, Red, was in the living room seated in his favorite chair and Chase was nowhere to be found. She sat on the sofa and smiled at her dad.

"I love family meals," he said. "I love having the family all together."

"It was nice," she agreed. As usual when speaking to her father she made her voice louder than usual. Although Red refused to admit any problem, all of his kids knew he was growing deaf. "It won't be long before the family gets bigger. Anna is pregnant and I have a feeling if Kate has her way she won't be far behind her."

Red's eyes took on a faraway cast. "Grandchildren are a blessing. I just wish—" He broke off and smiled at Meredith. "Well, you know what I wish."

She nodded. He wished Meredith's mother were here to share it all with him. He wished his wife were by his side in the autumn of their lives. Meredith thought of the file that was in the top drawer of her dresser in her bedroom.

She couldn't give her mother back to her father,

but maybe after all these years she could finally give him some closure. She could give him the name of Elizabeth's murderer.

Minutes later Kathy and Smokey came out of the kitchen and the four of them visited for another half hour or so. Chase came into the living room from his bedroom just about the same time Red decided to retire for the night.

By ten o'clock everyone had gone to his or her room except Chase and Meredith. "Is now a good time to go through that file?" he asked her.

"It's a perfect time. I'll just go get it." As she left the living room, she drew deep breaths, wondering what it was about Chase McCall's presence that made her feel as if she never got quite enough oxygen.

She retrieved the file from the dresser drawer, then returned to the living room. "Why don't we go into the kitchen where we can spread it out on the table?" she suggested.

He nodded and together they went into the kitchen and sat at the round oak table. Meredith placed her hand on the top of the file, for a moment feeling as if she were about to open Pandora's box.

Inside the folder was the last evidence of a life interrupted, the pieces of an investigation that had yielded no results, leaving a man and six children to wonder who had committed such outrage and left behind such devastation.

"You sure you want to do this?" Chase's voice

was soft, but his gaze was sharp and penetrating, as if he were attempting to look directly into her soul.

"No, I'm not at all sure I want to do this," she replied honestly. "But, I feel like I *have* to." She looked at the folder beneath her hand. "I feel like she wants me to do this, she needs me to do this." She laughed and looked at him once again. "I know it sounds crazy."

"No, it doesn't," he replied. "I know all about needing answers, but you realize it's possible we won't get the answers you want from that file."

"I know. I'm just looking for a lead, something that was perhaps overlooked when the initial investigation took place."

He pulled the folder from beneath her hand and opened it. He quickly withdrew three photographs and flipped them face down on the table just out of her reach. "There's no reason for you to see those," he said. There was a toughness in his tone that forbade her to argue with him.

She didn't want to argue. She didn't want to see crime-scene photos of her mother's broken body. She had a faint memory of her mother's smiling face, and she wanted nothing to displace her single visual memory of the woman who had given her life.

For the next hour they pored over the papers and while she read lab reports and crime-scene analyses she tried not to notice the evocative scent of Chase, the heat of his body so close to hers.

It had been a very long time since she'd been so

intensely aware of a man and aware of her own
desire for a man. She held no illusions about her desirability as a woman. She'd always been a bodyguard first, a woman second, more in touch with her
abilities to exist in a man's world than in her own
femininity.

But as she sat next to Chase, she wished she knew
more about womanly wiles, about how to flirt and
how to let a man know she was interested in him.

She instantly chided herself. She knew nothing
about Chase McCall, about what kind of man he
was, what was important to him. She knew nothing
about him except the fact that one glance of his
eyes and everything tightened inside her, one brush
of his hand against hers and the defenses she kept
wrapped around herself threatened to shatter.

With a sigh of irritation at her own wayward
thoughts, she consciously focused on the paper in
her hand.

"Was it your mother's usual habit to go grocery
shopping on a Friday night?" Chase asked.

"I don't know. Unfortunately, I don't know a lot
about my mother."

His eyes held curiosity. "You never asked your
father or any of your brothers about her?"

She leaned back in the chair and frowned thoughtfully. "Over the years I'd asked some simple questions. I wanted to know what kind of woman she was,
what she liked and didn't like. But I never asked
anything that might stir up Dad's grief all over again."

Chase nodded. "I'd be interested to know if your mother was a creature of habit or if the shopping trip that night was just a spur-of-the-moment thing."

"Maybe I should write down some of the questions." She got up from the table and went to the desk in the corner of the kitchen to get pen and paper. "Tanner would be the one for me to talk to. He was ten when Mom died and he still has a lot of memories of her."

It was a relief to have just that momentary distance from him, from his pleasant scent that seemed to fill her head. When she returned to the table, she noticed that the photos he'd placed on the side had been moved, letting her know that while she'd hunted for paper and pen, he'd looked at those photos.

He leaned back in the chair and frowned thoughtfully. "The investigation looks tight. The officials did everything that should have been done," he said. "Unfortunately they didn't have a lot to go on. There were no witnesses and not much evidence to examine. But it looks like they spoke to your mother's friends and acquaintances to see if there was anyone giving her problems or somebody she'd made angry." He shrugged. "It doesn't look like they missed anything."

Meredith sighed in frustration. She'd hoped he'd find something, anything that might provide a lead to the killer.

She stared toward the window where the black of night reflected her image back to her. "I think she was killed by somebody who knew her, somebody here in town. For a week after she was buried, a bouquet of daisies was placed on her grave. Daisies were my mother's favorite flowers and nobody from the family was responsible for putting them there. A bouquet of daisies is still put on her grave every year on the anniversary of her death."

"Has that been investigated?" He leaned forward, as if she'd captured his attention. His blond hair gleamed in the artificial light and she wondered if it was as soft as it looked.

She nodded. "Clyde Walker was the sheriff at the time of her death and he tried to solve the mystery of the daisies. According to Tanner what he discovered was that an FTD order was placed and paid for in cash from Oklahoma City directing the flowers be placed on the grave for that week. The florist here had no idea who had ordered them. Sheriff Ramsey has tried to get to the bottom of the yearly bouquets, but he hasn't learned anything new."

"I agree with you, I think she was killed by somebody she knew, by somebody she trusted."

"Why do you think that?" Meredith asked.

"The evidence, such as it is, supports it. I'm assuming that stretch of road between here and town is dark and probably not well traveled."

"That's right."

"There was no evidence in those reports that your mother had any kind of car trouble that night, yet she pulled over to the side of the road and got out of her car to meet her murderer. That's not consistent with a stranger kill. And there's something else…" He frowned, his gaze assessing, as if gauging how strong she was, how much she could hear.

She raised her chin and held his gaze. "Tell me. What else?"

He rubbed a hand across his lower jaw where she could see the faint stubble of a five-o'clock shadow. "According to the crime-scene report, there was evidence of a struggle and yet from the photo I saw that was taken when your mother was found, her clothing was almost artfully arranged in place. If I had to guess, whoever killed your mother had some sort of feelings for her."

He leaned forward and gathered the papers together and shoved them back into the folder, then looked at her once again. "Is it possible your mother was seeing somebody?"

"You mean like an affair? Absolutely not," she said forcefully. "Everyone who knew my parents talk about how devoted they were to each other. All of the women who knew my mother said she adored my father."

She didn't even want to think that the fairy-tale love her parents had shared wasn't true, that her mother had wandered outside her marriage vows. "Mom was a budding actress in Hollywood when she met Dad. She was just beginning to enjoy success and attention. She left her career behind to move here with him and have a family."

He tapped a finger on the file. "I don't see how I can help you on this," he said. "It looks like everything was done at the time to try to find the murderer. It's a cold case with no new evidence to explore."

"That's what I was afraid of," she replied. "I really appreciate your thoughts on this."

"No problem." He grinned, a slow, sexy gesture that caused her breath to momentarily catch in her chest. "Now, tell me, why don't you go to the town dances?"

She got up from the table. Now that he'd done what she'd wanted him to do in looking through the files, she felt the need to escape. The kitchen felt too small, his very presence far too big.

He rose from the table and moved to stand within inches of her. His clean, masculine scent once again infused her head, making her half-dizzy. "I thought all women loved dances," he said, his breath warm on her face.

"I went to a few but I got tired of standing around waiting for somebody to ask me to dance." *Step back,* her mind commanded, but it was as if her legs had gone numb.

"I find that hard to believe," he said, his gaze focused on her mouth. She fought the impulse to lick her lips, afraid he might see it as an open invitation, even more afraid she would mean it as an invitation.

"It's true," she said, the words seeming to come

from far away. "I don't know if the men in this town are more afraid of my brothers or because I carry a gun."

He touched her then, a mere brush of her hair away from her face. As his fingertips skimmed the side of her cheek, a coil of heat unfurled in the pit of her stomach.

"I've met all your brothers and I don't find them scary at all. And I carry a gun, too, so that definitely doesn't bother me. But, let me tell you what does bother me." His eyes were no longer cold and assessing, but rather warm and inviting. "It bothers me that since the moment I laid eyes on you I've wondered what your mouth would feel like under mine."

Her breath caught painfully tight in her throat. "Do you intend to keep on wondering or do you intend to find out?" Her heart crashed inside her chest.

How had they gotten from talking about a murder to contemplating a kiss? She didn't know and she didn't care. All she wanted at the moment was for him to kiss her…hard and deeply.

"I definitely intend to find out," he said as he wrapped her in his strong arms and pulled her tight against him. His mouth took hers, his lips possessing, demanding.

She opened her mouth to him, wanting the touch of his tongue against hers, the shattering heat of full possession. She raised her arms around his neck and placed her fingers where the bottom of his thick, silky hair met his shirt collar. Soft. The blond hair was definitely soft.

The kiss seemed to last forever, but it wasn't long enough for her. It was he who finally broke the kiss and stepped back from her, his eyes gleaming with wicked intensity.

"If you dance even half as well as you kiss, then we should have a great time on Saturday night." He walked over to the table and picked up the file folder. "Sweet dreams, Meredith," he said, then left the kitchen.

She stared after him, wondering if she'd ever breathe normally again. Meredith had spent most of her life competing with her brothers, but at this moment she was intensely grateful that she was a woman.

He'd seen the cars come and go at the West ranch from his hiding place in the stand of trees. The entire family had gathered. But he wasn't interested in any of the others…just *her*…just Elizabeth.

No, not Elizabeth, he told himself. Elizabeth was gone. Dead. But Meredith was wonderfully alive and having her would be like having Elizabeth.

It had only been in the last month or so that he'd realized that Meredith was the spitting image of the woman he'd loved, the woman he'd been obsessed with.

Before the last month, Meredith had been out of town a lot and he'd rarely run into her. Then one day he'd seen her walking on the sidewalk downtown, and he'd been electrified by the sight. It was as if Elizabeth walked again, breathed again.

He'd been unable to get Meredith out of his mind. She was so beautiful. He could almost feel the silk of her dark hair between his fingers. He wanted to drown in the green depths of her eyes. Just looking at her made it hard to breathe. She possessed his every thought.

He had to have her. His need soared through him, filling him with both a euphoric high and an edge of apprehension. He had to have her. He would have her, but this time he'd do things differently. This time he'd try not to kill her.

Chapter 4

The scents of popcorn, cotton candy and autumn rode the air as Chase got out of Red West's car. It had already been a full day with pie-eating, cattle-judging and jelly-tasting contests.

A carnival had taken up residency in the parking lot in front of the community center. Multicolored lights flickered on the Ferris wheel as the delighted screams of the riders competed with the raucous laughter coming from the Tilt-A-Whirl.

Soon the carnival would shut down and the night would belong to the adults of Cotter Creek. "It's a beautiful night," Kathy said as she and Smokey, Red and Chase walked toward the community building where the dance would be taking place.

It was a perfect autumn night. A full moon hung in a cloudless sky and it was unusually warm for early October.

"Mark my words, there will be mischief tonight," Smokey said gruffly as he looked up in the sky. "Add full-moon madness with a live band and liquor and there's sure to be trouble."

Maybe a little prefull-moon madness was what Chase had suffered two nights ago when he'd kissed Meredith. He hadn't begun the night with any intention of kissing her, but at the time of the kiss, he'd felt as if he *needed* to kiss her.

Even now, just the thought of the taste of her soft lips beneath his had the effect of heating his blood. He didn't like it. He didn't like it one bit. That kiss had shaken him up far more than he liked to admit.

Since the night of the kiss, he'd tried to keep his distance from Meredith, both mental and physical. Red had taken him into town each morning, and he'd caught a ride back to the ranch with Dalton in the evenings.

He'd spent a lot of time in the café, talking to the locals, trying to get a handle on the crimes that had brought him to Cotter Creek.

But he'd found the locals reluctant to talk to strangers. He was obviously viewed as an outsider in the small tight-knit community. The only person who seemed to talk fairly freely was old man Sam Rhenquist who stationed himself every morning on the bench outside the barbershop. Although initially the old man had been fairly closemouthed, the more time Chase spent seated on the bench with Sam, the more the man seemed inclined to talk.

Chase and Dalton had spent the night before slugging back beers and shooting pool at the local bar. Every minute he spent with his friend produced a sick guilt inside him as he thought of how he was deceiving him. But the tips pointing a finger at the Wests couldn't be ignored.

That morning he'd touched base with Agents Tompkins and Wallace to see what progress they'd made during their time in Cotter Creek. They were in the middle of investigating Sheila Wadsworth's life. Sheila Wadsworth was the real estate agent who had been responsible for the sales of the property to the MoTwin Corporation.

She'd been murdered, but the agents were hoping that in the reams of paperwork she'd left behind, they might find the identity of the local man or men behind the scheme. Unfortunately, they had little to report so far.

"I thought Meredith was coming with us tonight," Kathy said, the question pulling Chase out of his thoughts.

"She went over to Libby and Clay's and told me she'd meet us here later," Red replied.

As they entered the community building, a band was warming up on the stage and a group of young men stood nearby, most of them looking as if they'd already gotten their noses in the sauce. They snickered and elbowed one another as they eyed the women who crossed their path.

Red, Smokey and Kathy sat at one of the tables that ringed the dance floor while Chase spied Dalton across the room and excused himself to join his friend.

"If I didn't know better, I'd swear you were nothing but an Oklahoma cowboy," Dalton said with a grin.

Chase fingered the pearl buttons on his western-style black shirt. "Mom bought this for me this afternoon and insisted I wear it tonight."

"I'd expect you to have a black hat hanging on the wall and a black horse waiting for you in the parking lot."

Chase grinned. "Only it would be a white hat and a white horse. Have you forgotten that I'm one of the good guys?"

Dalton laughed and clapped him on the back, and once again a wave of guilt shot through Chase. He hoped he could complete this assignment and get back to Kansas City and Dalton would never know about his role in investigating the West family.

"I thought you had a date tonight," Chase said.

"I do. I've got to go pick her up in half an hour. In the meantime, how about I buy you a beer?" Dalton gestured toward the cash bar in one corner.

"You know me, I never turn down a beer."

The two men got their drinks, then joined the rest of the family at the table where Smokey and Kathy were arguing about what ingredients made the best coleslaw dressing.

Chase had learned quickly that Smokey Johnson was a stubborn, opinionated old cuss, but as he watched Kathy hold her own, he suspected the old man had met his match. He'd never seen his partner look quite so animated.

She had dressed up for the evening, wearing a blue dress that sharpened the blue of her eyes, and a touch of blush colored her cheeks. She looked like a small-town woman eager for a night of fun rather than the seasoned FBI agent she was.

People continued to arrive, everyone looking as if they'd donned their Sunday best for the dance. He wasn't surprised to see Bill Wallace and Roger Tompkins arrive. He didn't acknowledge the fellow FBI agents' presence in any way.

The band began to play and within minutes the dance floor was filled with twirling couples. "I think it would be nice if you asked me to dance," Kathy said to Smokey.

He looked at her as if she'd lost her mind. "Dancing is for kids."

She smiled and stood, her hand extended to him. "You're only as young as you feel, and right now I feel like a kid."

"But I've got a bum leg," Smokey protested.

"And I have arthritis. I figure we can lean against each other and make it around the dance floor."

Smokey looked helplessly around the table, as if

seeking some kind of support. Red offered a benign smile and Dalton merely shrugged his shoulders.

"You might as well go ahead," Chase said. "When she gets her mind made up about something, she doesn't take no for an answer."

With a frown that would have daunted most women, Smokey rose to his feet and took Kathy's hand. She was really working it, Chase thought. It wouldn't be long before Smokey Johnson didn't have a thought in his head that Kathy didn't know about. If he had anything to do with the death of the ranchers and the land scheme, Kathy would ferret it out.

Before the dance had ended, Zack and his wife, Kate, and Tanner and his wife, Anna, arrived and joined them all at the table.

Chase was beginning to wonder if perhaps Meredith wasn't coming, that maybe his indifference to her the past couple of days had made her change her mind. That was fine with him. He didn't like the hunger she stirred in him.

He saw Sam Rhenquist across the room and walked over to speak to the old man. "Hello, Sam."

"Chase." He nodded his head.

"How you doing this evening?"

"Same as I do every evening. My bones ache, I worry about world peace and heart palpitations and wonder if I'll wake up in the morning."

"I have a feeling you have lots of mornings left," Chase replied. "Good turnout for tonight."

"Nothing this town likes better than a party, especially after all that's happened the last couple of months."

Chase looked at him with speculation. "I figure a man who parks himself on Main Street for most of the day hears things, maybe sees things that others don't hear or see. What do you know about what's been going on?"

Sam looked at him for a long moment, his brown eyes wary. "I reckon I know that the last person who opened her mouth to talk about what was going on here in town wound up dead." He didn't wait for Chase to respond but instead walked off in the direction of the cash bar.

Meredith stood just outside the door to the community center, trying to get up her nerve to go inside. She hadn't been to a town dance in several years, but that wasn't what made her nerves dance in her stomach like overactive jumping beans.

Never had she dressed the way she looked this evening. Never had she put on makeup the way she had tonight. She had no idea what had gotten into her when she'd chosen to borrow the emerald-green dress from Libby.

Okay, she had a little bit of an idea. She suspected it had been irritation with Chase McCall that had prompted her to pick a dress that showed more cleavage than she'd ever displayed and hugged curves she hadn't even known she possessed.

As she thought of Chase, a new flash of irritation

swept through her. The man had kissed her, then ditched her. He'd seemed to go out of his way over the past two days to avoid her, and that had fed every single insecurity she had as a woman.

Tonight, for the first time in her life, she'd wanted to look like a woman. She smoothed the silky green material over her waist, then drew a deep breath and stepped into the crowded community center. She was going to try her best to act like a woman.

It didn't take her long to find the table her family had commandeered. As she approached, she was aware of several of the men eyeing her up and down and equally aware of the scowls that suddenly decorated her brothers' faces.

"Did you forget to put on the rest of that dress?" Zack asked darkly when she reached the table.

Kate elbowed him hard in the ribs. "Shush up," she demanded, then smiled at Meredith. "You look absolutely stunning."

Tanner frowned. "Any of those drunken cowboys make a move toward you, then I'll be spending the night kicking some cowboy butt."

Meredith sighed and sat next to Anna, Tanner's wife. "This is why I never come to these things. There's nothing worse for a woman's social life than overprotective brothers. Where's Smokey?"

Anna pointed to the dance floor where Smokey and Kathy were dancing. "Aren't they cute?" Anna said. "This is their third dance."

Meredith nodded, shocked at the smile that

curved Smokey's mouth upward. She wasn't sure she could remember the last time Smokey had smiled so much.

Everyone was accounted for except Dalton and Chase, not that she cared where Chase might be.

She'd only been seated for a few minutes when Buck Harmon walked over to her. "Evening, Meredith." He nodded to everyone else at the table, his gaze darting first left, then right with obvious nervousness. "I was wondering if you'd like to dance with me."

At forty years old Buck was a divorced man. He was nice, but with his long, pointed nose and small eyes he'd always reminded Meredith of a ferret.

"I'd love to dance," she replied and stood.

"Just don't hold her too close," Zack warned, and Buck's face changed to the color of a ripened tomato.

"'Course not," he replied.

Meredith shot her brother a dirty look, then allowed herself to be led onto the dance floor.

"You look real pretty tonight," Buck said as he held her at a respectable distance from him. "I don't believe I've ever seen you look so pretty."

"Thanks," she replied.

"I'm cutting in." The deep familiar voice came from behind Meredith. Buck instantly dropped his hand from her waist and stepped back as Chase dismissed him as if he were nothing but an irritating fly.

He took her hand and pulled her into his embrace with a possessiveness that renewed her irritation with him. It didn't help that he looked positively amazing in his black shirt and tight jeans.

"What makes you think I wanted you to cut in?" she asked peevishly.

He smiled, but the gesture didn't quite reach the depths of his eyes. "Because you had the look of a deer in the headlights. That guy wasn't your type at all."

"And you are?" He smelled wonderful, a hint of shaving cream and woodsy cologne. An utterly male scent that seemed to envelop her.

"I am for the length of this dance." He pulled her closer, so close her nose came precariously close to his shoulder. "Was it your intention to start a riot tonight?"

She leaned back and looked at him once again. "What are you talking about?"

"I'm talking about that dress." His eyes now held a hint of emotion, something dangerous and simmering just beneath the surface that caused her heart to beat erratically.

"What's wrong with my dress?"

This time there was no mistaking the spark that lit his eyes. "Absolutely nothing." Once again he pulled her closer. "You've got every man in this room wanting you and every woman in the room hating you." His voice warmed the air near her ear.

A breathless wonder filled her. Was being a desirable woman really as simple as putting on a form-fitting dress and a little bit of makeup? Was this all that it would have taken to make Todd happy?

Somehow she didn't think so. Besides, the wonder was short-lived as she thought of how Chase had avoided her after kissing her.

"I've never much cared what people thought of me," she replied with a touch of coolness to her tone.

"Does that include me?" he asked.

"You're at the top of my I-don't-care list."

He laughed, as if he didn't believe her, as if he could feel the throb of her heartbeat against his muscled chest. *It's true,* she told herself. *I don't care anything about Chase McCall. He'll only be in my life for the length of his vacation, then he and his mother will be gone.*

But as his muscled thigh pressed against hers and his hand tightened around her back, she found it hard to convince herself that he didn't affect her on any level.

He danced well. He was a strong lead and managed to make her feel graceful as he moved her around the dance floor.

"You're angry with me," he said.

"Why on earth would I be angry with you?" she countered.

"Maybe because I haven't spent any time with you the past couple of days. Maybe because I kissed you and have barely talked to you since then. Or maybe because I haven't kissed you again." His eyes sparked with a touch of humor.

"Get over yourself," she scoffed. "What are you doing, Chase, looking for some excitement by playing head games with me? Bored with your vacation? Might I suggest you enter a local bull-riding contest to alleviate any boredom you might be suffering."

He laughed again, then sobered. "I'm not trying to play head games with you." His gaze intensified. "I'll admit that I'm very attracted to you and there's nothing I'd like more than to act on that physical attraction, but I'm not looking for any kind of relationship so I figured it was best if I backed away."

"And what makes you think I'm interested in any kind of relationship except a physical one?" she asked, surprised at how his blatant confession of wanting her thrilled her.

He looked at her in surprise. "Because every woman I've ever known wants more than just a couple of rolls in the hay from a man."

"I've been told on more than one occasion that I'm not like most women," she replied. At that moment the music ended and she stepped out of his embrace. "Thanks for the dance, cowboy. The next move is up to you." With these bold words she turned and walked away.

She went directly toward the ladies' room, unable to believe her own audacity. She'd practically given him an open invitation to seduce her. What on earth had gotten into her?

As she stood at one of the sinks and dabbed her warm cheeks with a damp paper towel, she realized exactly what had gotten into her. Loneliness.

Other than Savannah, Meredith had no close friends. Savannah was warm and funny and great to spend time with, but she wasn't a significant other. She wasn't what Meredith was lonely for…a man.

The brief relationship she'd had with Todd seemed like another lifetime ago and in the short time that she'd been with Todd she'd discovered that she liked sex. Of course, at the time she was having sex with Todd she'd believed they were building toward an *I do*. Instead he'd been working up his nerve to tell her *No thanks*.

At least if she decided to have a physical relationship with Chase she'd have no illusions of how it would end. It would end with him going back to Kansas City and her no worse for the experience. Her loneliness would be alleviated for a short time, and that in itself was appealing.

She tossed the towel into the nearby trashcan and left the restroom. As she walked out, she was immediately greeted by Doug Landers, a man who'd been a classmate all through school.

"Meredith," he said and slung an arm around her shoulder. He smelled like too little deodorant and too much whiskey. "Darling, who knew that beneath those ugly shirts and jeans you wear was the body of a goddess?"

"Let me go, Doug. You're drunk," she exclaimed.

"I'm not too drunk to appreciate a fine piece of ass when I see it," he replied.

She tried to move away from him, but he tightened his arm around her. She was vaguely aware of Chase coming out of the men's room. As he saw her, his pleasant expression transformed into something dark and dangerous.

"Doug, I'm warning you, let me go," she exclaimed.

The drunken cowboy laughed, his breath potent enough to stop a raging bull in its tracks. "I'm not letting you go until I get a little kiss."

Meredith acted purely on instinct. In one smooth move she grabbed his arm from her shoulder, whirled out of his embrace and yanked his arm up behind his back.

He yelped in pain. "Let me go, you bitch," he exclaimed.

She gave his arm a final yank upward, then released him and pushed him away. As he stumbled off, she saw the stunned surprise on Chase's face and she felt slightly sick to her stomach.

She had a feeling this was exactly what Todd had been talking about, her inability to allow a man to help her, her lack of helplessness and charming softness that every woman was supposed to embody.

Suddenly tired, all she wanted to do was go home. It depressed her, the fact that she knew how to be a great bodyguard but didn't know anything about being a woman.

"I'd ask if you were okay, but it's obvious you can take care of yourself," Chase said as he approached.

"Growing up with all my brothers, I had to learn

a little self-defense," she said as they walked in the direction of the table. To heck with her promise to Dalton to babysit his friend, she thought crossly. "I think I'm going to head home. I've had enough Fall Festival for one year."

"But I've only gotten to dance with you once," he said. "Are you sure you're okay?" he asked, a touch of concern darkening his eyes.

"I'm fine. Just tired." They reached the table and she said her goodbye to her family, then grabbed her purse and headed for the nearest exit.

As she wove through the people to reach the door, she was aware of Doug's malevolent glare following her progress. He was obviously angry with her, but he'd probably get over it when he sobered up.

She hadn't realized how noisy it was inside until she stepped out the door and into the still night. The unusually warm air wrapped around her, banishing the last of Chase's scent that had lingered in her head.

Maybe a brief, hot affair was exactly what she needed. No expectations. No disappointments. Just a momentary respite from her loneliness.

Pulling her keys from her purse, she realized she couldn't wait to get out of the dress, couldn't wait to wash the makeup off her face. She'd tried to be something she wasn't this evening, and she wouldn't make that mistake again.

Eventually she might find a man who cared about her, who could fall in love with her as she was, and if that didn't happen, then she would live her life alone.

As she approached her car she frowned, noticing something white sticking out from under the driver's windshield wiper. When she got closer she saw it was a piece of paper folded several times. She plucked it out and opened it.

"I've been waiting for you for a very, very long time. You are my destiny."

The words were printed in block letters and the note wasn't signed. She unlocked her car door and slid behind the steering wheel, the note clutched in her hand.

The creepy feeling returned, raising the hair on the nape of her neck, dancing goose bumps along her arms. A secret admirer?

Maybe some women would be thrilled by the very idea. Meredith wasn't. She didn't like secrets. She looked around the parking lot, seeking the source of the note. But while the lot was crowded with cars and trucks, she saw nobody standing in the shadows, nobody crouched down next to a car.

She tucked the note into her purse, started her car engine, then on instinct did something she'd never done before in Cotter Creek. She locked her car doors.

Chapter 5

Chase awakened late the next morning with the hangover from hell. A long hot shower eased most of his misery, and by the time he left his room he suffered only an irritating headache that he hoped a gallon of coffee would banish.

He rarely drank too much. He had far too many memories of his old man, drunk and mean, and a deep-seated fear that at any minute he might become the same kind of man.

But last night after Meredith had left the dance, he'd drunk to forget how good she'd felt in his arms. He'd drunk to erase the feel of her long, slender legs against his, the press of her breasts against his chest and the challenge in her eyes when she'd told him that the next move was up to him.

He'd just come down the hall and into the living room when he heard a knock on the front door. Seeing nobody else around he walked to the front door. A young man stood on the porch clutching a long, white florist box.

"I have a delivery for Meredith West," he said.

"I'll take it." Chase took the box, gave the kid a tip, then closed the door and went to hunt down Meredith. It was obvious somebody had sent Meredith flowers. It surprised him how much he didn't like the idea. However, it didn't surprise him that she'd managed to garner some man's attention the night before.

She'd looked hot, and the fact that she'd seemed unaware of just how good she looked had made her even hotter. Holding her in his arms had been an exquisite form of torture. Flirting with her had been stimulating, but nothing had prepared him for her giving him the go-ahead for a lusty, no-commitment-necessary relationship.

It had been the burn of desire deep in his gut that he'd tried to anesthetize after she'd left the dance. But no amount of beer had been able to vanquish the simmering heat she'd stirred in him.

He found her in the kitchen with Smokey and Kathy. The three of them were seated at the table, drinking coffee and chatting about the dance the night before.

"These are for you," he said as he entered the kitchen. This morning there was no red lipstick decorating her full, sensual lips, no mascara to darken her long, dark eyelashes. She didn't appear to have on a stitch of makeup, but she had a face that didn't need artificial enhancements.

Once again she was clad in a red flannel shirt and jeans, but he couldn't help but remember the creamy skin beneath the shirt, the full breasts the material couldn't quite hide.

Her eyes widened with a flare of pleasure as he set the box in front of her on the table. "For me?" she said in obvious surprise. She smiled, a gorgeous upturn of lips that renewed the burn in his stomach. He realized she might think the flowers had come from him.

"They were delivered just a minute ago," he said. The pleasure in her eyes dimmed a tad, and he suddenly wished he'd bought the flowers for her.

"Open it up," Kathy said with excitement. "Let's see what you've got."

Chase poured himself a cup of coffee, then joined them at the table as Meredith pulled off the top of the box to reveal a dozen long-stem, deep-coral-colored roses.

"Oh my, those are lovely," Kathy exclaimed. "Smokey, why don't you get her a vase?"

As Smokey got up from the table, Red came in the back door. "Who got the roses?"

"I did," Meredith replied.

"Who sent them?" He walked over to the sink to wash his hands.

Meredith frowned. "I don't know. There doesn't seem to be a card."

Red dried his hands on a towel, then joined them at the table. "Coral roses. That color means desire. I'd say you have an amorous new suitor."

Chase didn't like the sound of that, and from the expression on Meredith's face she wasn't overly thrilled. "I'd like to know who the suitor is. I don't like mysteries." She carried the box of roses to the counter where Smokey had filled a large crystal vase with water.

He watched as she arranged the roses, sticking them helter-skelter into the vase. Kathy jumped up from the table. "Here, honey, let me help you with that."

When the two rejoined everyone at the table, the talk once again turned to the dance the night before and the crime investigation taking place by the two FBI agents.

"I heard they were interested in Sheila Wadsworth's husband. You know he wasn't from around here," Red said. "I'd like to think that whoever is behind all this is somebody who isn't a neighbor or friend."

Chase tried to stay focused on the conversation, but a part of his brain was trying to figure out who might have sent the roses to Meredith.

"Whoever is behind it should have their hearts

torn out," Smokey said, his grizzled brows tugged together in a frown.

"My fear is that before this is all said and done, it's going to tear this town apart. Everyone is suspecting somebody else and those suspicions are going to hurt friendships," Red said.

Chase took a sip of his coffee, then said, "While I've been spending time in town, I've heard a few people who think you or one of your sons might be behind this land scheme."

"That's crazy," Meredith exclaimed.

Red laughed. "That doesn't surprise me." He leaned back in his chair. "Funny thing about being successful, seems along with the money and such, you manage to gain more enemies."

"There's a few in town who would love to see the West family fall," Smokey said. "Jealous, that's all they are, just pure jealous."

"Besides, what would I have to gain by being the mastermind of such a thing?" Red continued, "I've got enough money to keep my children and their children living in comfort for the rest of their lives. I own more land now than I'll ever know what to do with. I figure when you're investigating a crime the best way to solve it is to look for motive. Neither my children nor I have a good motive."

Chase took another sip of his coffee. He believed Red West. He'd only been in the bosom of the West family for less than a week, but he had found them all to be men of integrity.

He had a gut feeling that the tips that had been phoned in pointing a finger at the West family had been an attempt to lead the FBI on a wild-goose chase.

When they'd finished coffee and everyone had taken off in different directions, Chase waylaid Kathy and pulled her into his bedroom.

"My gut tells me we're wasting our time here," he said.

"I'm certainly not prepared to make that same assessment," she replied with a hint of stubbornness he recognized all too well. "I think it would be a big mistake to pull out of here too early."

Chase wasn't sure, but for some reason he felt like it was time to go, that they could be used better somewhere else, on another assignment. He had the distinct feeling that if they stuck around too much longer, things were going to get complicated between him and Meredith.

The adage of familiarity breeding contempt wasn't working for him. Each moment he spent near Meredith stoked the flames in his stomach a little hotter. "Kathy, the only thing we're gaining from sticking around here is that you're getting more recipes from that cranky old man," he said with a touch of irritation.

"Don't be disrespectful," Kathy exclaimed. "That cranky old man stepped in to fill a void formed from grief. He's done nothing but give to this family at the expense of him having his own life."

Chase stepped back, surprised by Kathy's quick

defense of the crotchety cook. Pink leaped to her cheeks. "All I'm saying is that we're in a perfect position as guests of the Wests to not only investigate them but to also hear local gossip and keep an eye on other townspeople," she said.

He suspected her interest in remaining here wasn't all about the job, but he didn't call her on it. "Okay," he relented. "We stick around another week or so and see what we can come up with."

She nodded and left his room. Chase walked over to the bedroom window and stared outside. What Red West said made sense. The Wests owned more land than they needed and had an incredibly successful business. Why would any of them want to become involved in some murderous land scheme?

Although prosecution of any crime didn't require the authorities to prove motive, Chase believed too that to solve a crime one had to look at motive. And as far as he was concerned, the Wests had none.

Sam Rhenquist knew more than he was saying about what was going on. The old man sat on that bench on Main Street day after day, watching and listening to the people who passed by. He knew more than he was telling, but he was afraid of the consequences should he talk. Chase wanted to make him talk.

And who in the hell had sent those roses to Meredith?

He heard the door across the hallway close, then

soft footsteps leading away. Meredith. He turned away from the window and left his bedroom, knowing he was walking in her wake by the faint scent of her perfume that lingered in the air.

He found her in the living room talking to her father. "I was just telling Dad that I'm headed into town. I have a lunch date with Savannah," she said.

"Mind if I catch a ride?" he asked.

"Suit yourself," she replied with a terse tone. She looked at him with a cool distance that made him wonder what was going on in her gorgeous head.

As he followed her to her car, he thought once again about the roses she'd received that morning and the look of both surprise and sheer pleasure that had lit her eyes.

It had been obvious that she wasn't accustomed to getting flowers. It irritated him that there was a small part of him that wished he'd sent them, that he'd been the one who had brought that smile of pleasure to her face.

"You have any idea who sent you the roses?" he asked when they were in her car and headed into town.

"Not a clue," she replied with a dark frown.

"Kind of romantic, huh," he said.

"Kind of creepy, if you ask me. If somebody feels desire for me, I prefer to know their name."

"Allow me to introduce myself," he said half teasing.

She didn't reply, but a faint pink stained her cheeks. They rode the rest of the way in silence. He tried several times to begin a conversation but she didn't respond and he finally gave up.

Just like a woman to get all moody and the man not to know what he'd done, he thought. Maybe it was a good thing that she seemed irritated with him. He had a feeling Kathy was getting far too close to Smokey Johnson. His partner was allowing her heart to get all twisted up, and as far as Chase was concerned that was always a mistake.

Chase didn't have a heart to get involved with anyone. A father who had professed to love him had beaten the heart right out of him. His biggest, deepest fear was that if he allowed himself to love somebody he'd turn out just like his old man and would eventually beat the heart right out of her.

Meredith and Chase parted ways in front of the hardware store. "If you want a ride back to the ranch, I'll be leaving around two," she said. She half hoped he'd find another way back to the ranch.

She needed to think. She needed to think about the note that had been left on her car the night before and the roses that had arrived that morning.

And she needed to think about Chase McCall and the bits and pieces of conversation she'd overhead him having with his mother.

Checking her watch, she realized it was too early to go to the newspaper office to meet Savannah. She had half an hour to kill before she was to meet her friend at eleven. She thought about heading to the

Wild West Protective Services office, but suspected that's where Chase had been headed. And what she needed at the moment was as much distance as possible from him.

Instead she crossed the street toward the direction of the floral shop, thinking that just maybe she could learn the identity of her secret admirer.

Cotter Creek Floral Creations was owned and operated by Mary Lou Banfield, a woman who had been one of Meredith's mother's closest friends.

A tiny bell tinkled cheerfully as Meredith entered the shop. The cloying scent of a variety of flowers hung in the air, each one fighting for dominance.

Mary Lou greeted her with a warm, friendly smile. "I wondered how long it would take this morning before I'd see you in here. The minute Joe carried those roses out of here for delivery, I knew sooner or later you'd show up."

"There was no card with the roses," Meredith said as she walked over to the counter where Mary Lou was making an arrangement of multicolored carnations and greenery.

"Whoever sent them didn't want you to know. It was a cash order written up and left in my mail slot this morning. The order was specific, a dozen orange roses sent to you, no card. I didn't have orange, but figured coral was close enough. Whoever ordered them overpaid by five dollars."

This information certainly did nothing to alleviate the unease that had gripped Meredith since the moment she'd opened the box of roses. "You still have the note that came with the money?" she asked.

Mary Lou nodded and opened the cash register. "Like I said, I figured you'd be in so I didn't throw it away."

Meredith took the piece of paper from her and read it. It was written in block letters just like the note she'd received beneath her windshield wiper the night before. It simply said, "Deliver to Meredith West one dozen long-stem orange roses." It was written on plain white bonded paper.

"I'd say you've got yourself a secret beau," Mary Lou exclaimed.

"I don't like secrets," Meredith replied. "I figure a real man doesn't stand behind anonymity."

Mary Lou smiled and picked up a bright-red carnation. "Your mother would have been so proud of you. You're just like her, strong and forthright. She was delighted you know, when you came along. Oh, she loved her boys but she desperately wanted a daughter. When you were born she told me that she'd just given birth to a person she hoped would become her very best friend."

A lump of emotion crawled into Meredith's throat as she realized again all she had lost when somebody had taken her mother's life. She swallowed hard against the lump. "Mary Lou, you probably knew my mother better than anyone in town. Do you think it was possible she was having an affair at the time of her death?"

"Who on earth have you been talking to that would put such nonsense in your head?" Mary Lou asked scornfully. "Elizabeth loved your daddy with every fiber of her being. She'd no more have an affair than she would have flown to the moon."

Even though Meredith hadn't seriously contemplated the affair angle, Mary Lou's staunch support of her mother was comforting. "I've been thinking about her a lot lately," Meredith said.

Mary Lou reached out and covered Meredith's hand with hers. "I miss her, too. She was a wonderful friend."

Meredith nodded, then withdrew her hand. "I've got to get out of here. I'm meeting Savannah for lunch."

"When are her and Joshua gonna tie the knot?"

"I don't know, they haven't set a date."

Mary Lou grinned. "It seems like every other month or so there's another West wedding to attend."

"You don't have to worry about me following in my brothers' footsteps. I can't even get a man who might be interested in me to sign a card."

"Maybe he's just shy. I'm sure when the time is right your secret admirer will reveal himself to you."

"I suppose," she replied, then with a goodbye she left the florist shop and headed toward the newspaper office to meet Savannah.

So, somebody shy had left her a note and sent her roses. There was no reason for her to feel anxious about it. Like Mary Lou had said, surely *eventually* he'd reveal himself to her.

Raymond Buchannan, the owner of the *Cotter Creek Chronicles* frowned as she walked into the office. "One hour, that's what Savannah's lunch break is supposed to be. Last time you two put your heads together over at the café she was an hour late back from lunch."

"I'll make sure that doesn't happen again," Meredith exclaimed. "I know how busy she is with all the news stories that are breaking minute by minute in this one-horse town."

Raymond's scowl deepened. He obviously had recognized her sarcasm. Savannah danced out of her office. "Right on time. I'll be back later, Mr. Buchannan," she said airily as she pulled Meredith out the front door.

"I don't know how you put up with him," Meredith said when the two hit the sidewalk. "He's so cranky."

Savannah linked arms with her. "I'll let you in on a little secret. I'm not going to have to put up with him too much longer."

Meredith stopped in her tracks and stared at her friend. "Don't tell me you're quitting your job. You love being a reporter."

"Of course I'm not quitting." Savannah pulled her into motion again. "But he's only going to be my boss until we can draw up the contracts."

Once again Meredith halted and looked at Savannah in surprise. "He's selling the paper to you?"

Savannah's freckled face wreathed into a smile. "Isn't it great? He's retiring and leaving town. We came to an agreement last night, and we're meeting with a lawyer tomorrow afternoon."

"Raymond has been talking about retiring for years, but nobody took him seriously," Meredith replied.

"I know. I was stunned when he approached me and told me it was time, that he was ready to pack his bags and let go of the paper."

"What does Joshua think about all this?"

"He thinks I'm crazy to want all the work and responsibility, but he's being totally supportive. I sometimes feel like I'm the luckiest woman in the world to have him."

The two entered the café and found a booth in the back. "Now, tell me what's new with you," Savannah said once the waitress had departed with their orders. "How's that hunky houseguest of yours? I've got to tell you, you two looked like you were going to combust last night on the dance floor."

Meredith suddenly remembered the conversation she'd overheard before she'd left the house. "I'm not sure I trust my hunky houseguest."

"From the way he looked at you last night, I wouldn't trust him, either. That man had lust in his heart."

"I'm not talking about that," Meredith said, although a tiny rivulet of heat swept over her as she thought about the way Chase's eyes had simmered as he'd held her in his arms. She'd never known blue eyes could look so…so…hot.

She grabbed a napkin and twisted it with her fingers. "I think he's not just here for a little friendly visit with Dalton."

Savannah frowned. "What do you mean?"

"I overhead a little of a conversation between him and Kathy this morning. First of all, he called her Kathy. Don't you find it odd for a man to call his mother by her first name?"

Savannah shrugged. "Not really. I mean, I call my mother The Monster."

"That's different," Meredith replied. "From everything you told me about your mother, she deserves to be called The Monster. But it's more than that. I could have sworn I heard Chase say something about being here on assignment."

Savannah frowned once again. "Isn't he a Kansas City cop? What kind of an assignment would bring him here?"

"I don't know. But I'm going to find out."

"How are you going to do that?"

Meredith took a sip of her water. "I'm going to ask him."

Savannah narrowed her eyes and studied Meredith intently. "Are you sure you aren't just looking for a reason to push him away?"

Meredith opened her mouth to vehemently protest, but instead closed it again. Was that what she was doing? She couldn't be absolutely certain she'd overheard correctly. Was she unconsciously looking for a reason to put distance between herself and Chase?

"I don't know," she finally admitted. "He scares me a little bit. He has a way of looking at me that makes me feel both wonderful and afraid."

Savannah nodded. "I know exactly what you're talking about. I feel the same way with Joshua."

"It's not the same," Meredith scoffed. "I'm not about to fall in love with Chase McCall." At that moment the waitress arrived with their orders.

Thankfully, the conversation as they ate revolved around the newspaper and Raymond Buchannan's decision to sell the paper to Savannah.

By the time they'd finished eating and Savannah had to get back to work, Meredith had managed to put thoughts of Chase on the back burner.

She didn't tell Savannah about the note and the roses. In fact, she hadn't told anyone about the note she'd found. She certainly didn't want to tell any of her family members, and Savannah would make a big deal out of it.

Savannah was the kind of woman who would think it was all wonderfully romantic. There was no way Meredith could explain to anyone the strange feeling of disquiet the note evoked in her.

It was almost two when Meredith returned to her car.

There was no sign of Chase, but there was a piece of paper placed beneath the driver's windshield wiper. Her fingers trembled as she plucked it out and opened it.

"You will be mine forever."

She crunched up the note into her fist as her gaze shot around the street. There were people everywhere, hurrying down the sidewalks to their destinations, sweeping off the sidewalks in front of their places of business. But nobody paid any attention to her. Nobody appeared to be watching her.

She didn't know how long she stood there with the note clutched tightly in her grip. This didn't feel like a secret admirer. It felt darker, more dangerous.

It felt like stalking, like a sick obsession.

He watched from the storefront as she got into her car and drove away. He closed his eyes, for a moment overwhelmed with need. Elizabeth. His heart cried out the name.

The afternoon sunshine had caressed her dark hair, and he wanted it to be his hands tangling in the rich strands. He'd been too far away to see her facial expression when she'd read the note, but he could imagine the sparkle of her eyes, the sweet anticipation that had flooded through her.

Soon, he thought. It was a promise to her. Soon. It was a promise to himself.

Chapter 6

She waited until quarter after two, and when Chase didn't show up, she left and headed back to the ranch. As she drove she tried to figure out who might be leaving the notes, who might have sent the roses.

Was it possible that Buck Harmon was responsible? He was the only man other than Chase who had asked her to dance. Had that brief moment in Buck's arms stirred something in the man?

Maybe she was overreacting to the whole situation. Maybe she should just sit back and enjoy the fact that she'd captured the interest of someone.

Like Mary Lou had said, when the time was right the man would identify himself. In the meantime there was no point in stewing about it.

As she thought of the florist she couldn't help but think about her mother. She liked to believe that if Elizabeth had lived she and Meredith would have been best friends.

By the time she pulled up at the house, she was hungry for a connection, any connection with her mother. If Elizabeth had lived, would she have taught Meredith the nuances of being a woman? A real woman?

She found her father where he usually was, out in his garden pulling weeds. He straightened as he saw her, a flash of pain creasing his features. The arthritis that had finally forced him to give up working for the family business seemed to grow more pronounced everyday. "Hey, girl. I thought you were in town."

"I just got back." She sat on a nearby stone bench and watched him once again begin to pull the weeds threatening to choke his fall-colored mums. "I've been thinking a lot lately about Mom."

Red smiled. "I think about her every single day." He brushed off his hands and joined Meredith on the bench. He smelled of earth and sunshine and that indefinable scent of Dad.

"I wish I could have known her. It's not everyone who can boast that her mother was a Hollywood starlet at one time."

Red laughed, a wistful sound of distant memories. "She was beautiful and she was a wonderful actress. She was on her way to stardom, and I couldn't believe it when she made the choice to give all that up to marry me and move out here in the middle of nowhere."

For a long moment he stared off into the distance, and Meredith knew he was remembering the woman he'd married, the woman he'd loved. He sighed, then looked back at Meredith. "You know there are boxes of your mom's Hollywood memorabilia in the old shed in the pasture."

"Really?" This was the first she'd ever heard of any boxes.

Red nodded. "Your mom packed that stuff out there and said those boxes were like her own personal time capsules. Maybe it's time you looked in them."

"I'd like that," she replied.

He stood. "I'll just go get the key to the shed."

Minutes later Meredith took off down the pasture lane. Once again it was an unusually warm day for October, but even the bright sun couldn't heat the cold places that the appearance of that second note had left inside her.

As she walked, her head swirled with disturbing thoughts. She apparently had a stalker, she had a houseguest who might not be who or what he claimed to be, and she had the haunting mystery of her mother's murder all battling for dominance.

The large shed was in the middle of nowhere with nothing but pasture around and in the distance groves of trees and other outbuildings. An overhang shielded bales of hay that were stored there and the other part of the shed was a typical locked storage area.

She unlocked the door and pushed it open, allowing the bright sunshine to add to the light coming in through a small window. Dust motes flew in the air, and she didn't even want to think about what spiders and bugs might be occupants.

The inside was stuffed with outcast furniture, old lamp fixtures and boxes. She moved around a sofa she never remembered seeing in the house and to a stack of boxes that were neatly labeled on the sides. She read the labels until she came to one that said Elizabeth.

With an effort, she pulled the box out from beneath several others, then carried it to the sofa. She sat down next to the box and opened the lid.

Playbills, old photographs and reviews greeted her, along with a swell of emotion for what might have been, what should have been. She should have had her mother in her life to guide her, to teach her, to love her.

How she wished she could find the sick bastard who had stolen that from her when he'd strangled the life out of her mother. What had Elizabeth West done to deserve being choked to death and left by the side of her car on a deserted road?

She picked up an old photograph and stared at the image. It was like looking into a mirror. She touched her mother's smile with the tip of her finger, and tears burned at her eyes.

She'd always thought it was impossible to mourn for something you'd never had, but she realized now that wasn't true. She mourned the mother she'd never had, mourned the girl talk and the hugs and kisses. In Meredith's world of five brothers, a father and Smokey, there had never been a soft place to fall. Her mother would have been that place, if she'd lived.

"Meredith."

The deep voice startled a cry from her, and she jumped up from the sofa, ready to defend herself from some unknown threat. She relaxed as she saw Chase standing in the doorway.

"What are you doing out here?" she asked. She sank back on the sofa as her heart resumed a more natural rhythm. She hadn't realized how on edge she'd been until he'd startled her.

"Your dad said you were out here going through some things of your mother's. I thought maybe if you were looking for clues you might need an extra pair of eyes." He walked over to the sofa and sat next to her.

"I'm pretty sure I won't find any clues out here to who might have murdered her. These boxes mostly contain things of my mother's from her days in Hollywood." She wished he hadn't sat so close to her, for his nearness created a tiny ball of tension in the pit of her stomach.

"What have you got there?" He pointed to the picture she held in her hand.

She held it out to him. "A picture of my mom."

"Wow, the resemblance is amazing." He looked from the picture to her, his gaze assessing. "Your hair is a little bit lighter and your face is a bit longer, but the differences are so subtle."

Meredith took the picture back from him and once again traced the smile with her fingertip. "I've read a few of the reviews of some of her work as an actress. She was as talented as she was pretty."

"Maybe you need to let it go," he said softly. She looked at him in surprise. "Maybe you need to let her go. Even if you solve her murder, it won't bring her back."

"I know that," she replied. She set the picture aside and sighed. "You don't know what it's like to grow up without a mother."

His eyes darkened, holding secrets. "I know what it's like to feel alone," he countered. "I know what it's like to feel isolated. Even though I had Kat…Mom, my childhood wasn't exactly a bag of chips."

She didn't miss his tongue bobble when he'd mentioned his mother, and it brought back the conversation she'd overheard that morning along with an edge of suspicion. "Who are you and what are you really doing here?"

His eyes narrowed slightly. "What do you mean?"

She stood, her gaze searching his features. "I think you know exactly what I mean. You aren't here on vacation, are you? There's something more. You and Kathy didn't just suddenly get a hankering to visit Dalton here in Cotter Creek. Tell me what you're really doing here."

He held her gaze for a long moment, a muscle ticking in his lower jaw. He finally broke the gaze and swiped a hand through his hair. "We're here on an investigation."

"An investigation?" She returned to the sofa and once again sat. "An investigation into what?"

"Into your family. We're looking into a couple of tips we got that somebody in your family is behind the land scheme and the death of those ranchers."

She stared at him in disbelief. She knew she should probably be angry, but she wasn't. She was somewhat relieved that her suspicions about him had proven correct. "So, you're what? FBI?" He nodded. "And Kathy?"

"Is my partner."

She sat back and tried to digest what she had just learned. "Does Dalton know?"

"No. Nobody knows except the two agents in town and now you. What gave us away?"

"I overheard some of a conversation you had with Kathy this morning," she replied. "I didn't mean to eavesdrop."

"But you did," he said flatly. "I don't suppose you'd consider keeping the information to yourself?"

"You know you're wasting your time. Nobody in my family would ever have anything to do with this," she said. "That's not the kind of people we are."

"We've pretty much come to that conclusion," he

replied. He reached and grabbed her hand in his, his gaze intent. "I'm asking you not to tell anyone about who we are and what we're doing here. We have a perfect cover as your guests to investigate people in this town."

She didn't like the way his hand felt holding hers, so warm and inviting. His scent filled the shed, a wonderful smell of male and wind and that woodsy cologne.

She pulled her hand from his. "I'll keep your secret for now," she agreed. "And I want you to investigate my family inside and out. I don't want there to be any doubt as to our innocence."

"Okay." He looked relieved.

"What's happening with the investigation? Any suspects?"

"Agents Wallace and Tompkins are still sifting through Sheila Wadsworth's papers and personal items, looking for a clue that might point a finger at somebody."

"So, basically, nothing is happening," she replied.

He frowned. "I think Sam Rhenquist knows something, but I can't get him to tell whatever it is he knows."

"That man gives *cranky* a new meaning."

"Yeah, well I tried to get him to talk to me this afternoon, but he was having nothing to do with it. Did you find out who sent you the roses?" he asked in an obvious attempt to change the subject.

"No. I went to the florist shop but didn't get any

answers. The order for the roses was left in the mail slot along with cash."

"You think maybe they were from that cowboy who tried to maul you outside the bathroom? Maybe some kind of apology for his behavior?"

She laughed and shook her head. "Doug is the kind of man who thinks it's funny to pass gas in church, he certainly doesn't have the class to send roses in apology for anything."

"You certainly put him in his place. That was a smooth move you did on him." There was a hint of admiration in his voice.

"I told you last night that you don't grow up with five brothers without learning the basics of self-defense, and in any case in my line of work I have to know how to take care of myself." And maybe that was the problem with her. Maybe that was why Todd hadn't wanted her, because she wasn't needy like a real woman should be.

"If I kissed you right now would you use some of that self-defense to fend me off?" he asked.

Her heartbeat stuttered. The last time he'd kissed her he'd taken her breath away, stirred a desire in her she'd never felt before. "I guess you won't know until you try. I did tell you last night at the dance that the next move was up to you."

His eyes fired with a familiar spark that lit something hot and hungry inside her. With a studied determination he stood and reached out to take her hand. He pulled her up off the sofa and into his arms.

She didn't even think about protesting. She'd wanted him to kiss her every moment of every day since he'd last kissed her. "You drove me crazy in that little green dress last night at the dance," he said as his arms tightened around her. "But you drive me just as crazy in your flannel shirt and jeans."

There was nothing else he could have said that would have effectively melted her as these words did. "Do you intend to just stand there, or do you intend to do something about it?" she asked.

"Oh, I definitely intend to do something about it." His mouth took hers in a kiss that demanded surrender, that took no prisoners.

And she surrendered. She opened her mouth to him as her knees weakened and she melted against the hard length of his body. His tongue rimmed her lower lip, then plunged inside to battle with her own.

Meredith wrapped her arms around his neck, wanting to feel the silk of his gorgeous blond hair, needing to mold herself to him.

There was no slow build. As he deepened the kiss, there was nothing but hot hunger ripping through her.

His hands moved up and down her back, heating her skin through the shirt's fabric, deepening the hunger in her for more—more intimacy, more tactile pleasure, more Chase.

She'd set the rules when she'd told him she wasn't interested in anything but a physical relationship with him. And that was still true, now more than ever.

He was an FBI agent, here for the moment but before long he'd be gone back to Kansas City and out of her life. She had no illusions, no expectations. All she knew was that she wanted this man right now.

He broke the kiss only long enough to move his mouth from her lips to her neck where he nipped and nibbled as if he couldn't get enough of the taste of her.

She gasped as his hands gripped her buttocks and pulled them against him. He was aroused, and the feel of his hardness thrilled her. She ran her hands up beneath his shirt, loving the feel of his warm skin over taut muscles. Her fingers encountered several ridges of skin, the telling feel of scars, and vaguely she wondered about them, but had no ability to process any rational thought.

He in turn moved his hands beneath her shirt, the heat of his hands warming her back, then making her gasp once again as he moved them around her body to cup her breasts. Once again his mouth took possession of hers and she was no longer capable of conscious thought.

His thumbs rubbed across the tips of her breasts, warming despite the barrier of her bra. Her nipples tightened and hardened as if to greet the touch.

She ground her hips against his, needy as she'd never been. As her fingers began to fumble at the buttons on his shirt, he caught her wrists in his hands and stepped back.

His ragged breathing filled the silence of the shed. "Not like this," he said when he finally found his voice. "I want you more than I've ever wanted a woman in my life, but not here in this dusty shed." He dropped her wrists and took another step backward. "I want you in a bed, Meredith. I want you naked between the sheets."

She didn't say a word, wasn't sure at the moment that she was capable of speech. Desire pooled like hot liquid in the pit of her stomach, and her limbs felt heavy with it.

He raked a hand though his hair, then looked at his wristwatch. "Dalton is picking me up in half an hour. I don't want this between you and me to be a fast, frantic groping in an old shed. If you want me like I want you, then come to my room tonight." He took a step toward the door and smiled. "I guess that means the next move is up to you."

He didn't wait for her reply but turned and exited the shed. Meredith stared after him. She wasn't sure what scared her more, the mysterious notes and the idea of an obsessed mystery man or Chase McCall, who she suspected had the power to shake up her life like it had never been shaken before.

Chase had no idea if Meredith would come to his room or not. He now sat on the edge of his bed clad only in a pair of boxers. It was almost eleven, and the rest of the occupants of the house had retired over an hour before.

If she didn't come to the room, then he had a feeling an ice-cold shower was in his very near future, for just thinking about making love to her had him painfully tense.

He'd spent the evening with Dalton, eating dinner in the café then heading to the bar to shoot some pool and enjoy a few beers. As usual he'd kept his eyes and ears open in hopes of seeing or hearing something that might point a finger of blame to the guilty party.

Agents Wallace and Tompkins had come in just as Dalton and Chase were getting ready to leave. The two men looked tired and nodded curtly to both Dalton and Chase before settling at a table and ordering drinks.

"I don't envy them their jobs," Dalton had said as they'd left the bar. Once again guilt had gnawed at Chase as he thought of how he'd deceived his friend.

He'd been concerned when he'd told Meredith the truth about himself. He hadn't known how she might react. He'd been pleased that she didn't intend to tell the rest of her family members that he was a viper among them. And he wasn't surprised by her easy belief in the integrity of her family members.

Stretching out on the bed, he thought about the Wests. In the times he'd seen them all together, the warmth and strength of the connection between them all had been undeniable.

Family. There had been a time in his distant past when he'd been hungry for family, for a loving connection to somebody, anybody besides the father who had twisted him inside and out.

Over the years he'd stuffed that need deep inside where it couldn't be trampled by false expectations or disappointments. Work had taken the place of family, work had filled the needs he might have once allowed himself. But being around the Wests stirred that old hunger to belong, to be loved.

He froze as a soft knock fell on his bedroom door. All thought of family fell away as he opened the door to see Meredith standing there. He pulled her into his room and closed the door, electrified by her very presence.

Instead of jeans and a shirt, she wore a navy-blue knee-length nightshirt. She smelled of night-blooming jasmine, and her eyes shone with both excitement and a hesitant self-consciousness.

He didn't say a word, but instead pulled her into his arms and lowered his mouth to hers, taking up where they had left off that afternoon in the shed.

The skin-to-skin contact of their bare legs, and the feel of her braless breasts against his chest sizzled desire through his veins. He couldn't remember ever wanting a woman as much as he wanted her. He wanted her naked and gasping beneath him, wanted her mewling with pleasure as she cried out his name.

He reached down and grabbed the bottom of her nightshirt and broke the kiss only long enough to pull the material up and over her head. He threw it to the floor as his gaze hungrily took in the sight of her, clad only in a pair of tiny navy panties.

She was beautiful, her body sleek and toned and her eyes holding the same hunger that burned inside him. She stepped out of her panties, and he tore off his boxers, then they tumbled to the bed as their mouths met again.

His hands cupped her breasts, thumbs playing over the hardened nipples. It was only when he replaced his thumbs with his mouth that she uttered her first sound, a low, deep moan that seemed to come from the very depths of her.

As he laved her breasts with his mouth, her hands danced up and down his back, kneading and softly scratching until he was half-mindless with pleasure.

He skimmed his hands down the flat of her abdomen, her skin silky and soft. As his hands moved farther down she tensed against him, as if anticipating the intimacy to come.

But he wanted her to have complete pleasure before he took his own. As far as he was concerned, there was nothing as stimulating as giving his partner her release.

He found the soft folds of her center. She was already moist and ready for him. As he caressed, she thrust her hips upward.

Her eyelids were half-mast and her eyes glittered as she wrapped her fingers around the length of him. He almost lost it then, almost gave in to his need to take her fast and hard. But he closed his eyes and fought for control.

The only sound in the room was their ragged

breathing, but as she stiffened against his fingers, she buried her face in his chest, shuddered and released a long, deep moan.

Before her shudders had completely passed, he rolled over, grabbed the foil package off the nightstand and opened it with trembling hands. Within seconds he had positioned himself between her thighs and slid into her.

She surrounded him, with her evocative scent, with her tight heat. He knew no matter how much he wanted to make this last, it wouldn't. It couldn't. She felt too good for him to maintain any kind of control.

He stroked into her fast…faster, and she met him thrust for thrust until he knew she was once again on the verge of release, until she cried out his name. It was only then that he allowed himself his own release.

Afterward he rolled over to the side of her, his heartbeat still crashing with speed. She lay on her back, her hair in wild disarray, her own chest rising and falling at an abnormal rate. He got up and quietly left the room to go to the bathroom in the hallway.

When he returned to his room she hadn't moved but she looked at him, her gaze slightly challenging. "I'm not a slut. I don't fall into bed with every man who comes into town."

"The thought didn't even enter my mind," he replied as he got back into bed.

"It's been over a year since I've been with any man," she said.

"It's been almost that long since I've been with

a woman," he replied. For several moments they lay side by side, not speaking.

When his heartbeat had slowed and drowsy contentment swept over him, he reached for her and pulled her into his arms. She relaxed against him, her head on his chest and one leg sprawled over his.

He breathed in the scent of her as he swept a hand through her thick, dark hair. "I love the way you smell," he said softly.

"I love the way you feel," she said, her voice almost a purr. Her hand moved up his chest, stopping as it encountered one of his scars. "How did you get this?" She raised her head and looked at him.

"I had a broken bottle thrown at me."

"Were you involved in a barroom brawl?"

He fought the emotion that crawled up the back of his throat. "No barroom, just our kitchen. I'd forgotten to take out the trash and my father lost his temper."

Her fingers were soft as silk against his skin. "Your father did this to you?" Her gaze held a slight touch of horror.

Chase refused to let the baggage of his past destroy the fragile happiness he felt at this moment. "I told you my old man wasn't exactly Father of the Year." He took her hand in his and raised it to his lips. "And the last thing I want to talk about right now is him. He's dead and the past is gone."

"Except the scars," she replied.

"And they don't even hurt."

She laid her head back on his chest, and once

again his fingers danced through her hair. She'd been a good lover. For some reason he hadn't expected her to be so giving and so incredibly passionate.

It was nice that they were both on the same page, that he could enjoy this, enjoy her without worrying about what she might expect from him. No emotional entanglements, that was his creed, his motto for living.

Once again she raised her head and looked at him, her green eyes giving nothing away, not allowing him anywhere inside her head. "How long are you planning on being here?"

"I'm not sure. If it were up to me I'd say it's time to pack our bags. I don't believe any of your family members are involved in the crimes we're investigating."

"Why? Because we're all so charming?"

"There is that," he said with a smile. "But there's also the fact that we've run background checks on all of you and investigated your personal finances, your family business and everything else that might point to criminal activities."

"I should be outraged," she replied. "But right now I don't have the energy."

"Look at it this way, the suspect pool is considerably smaller if we remove all the Wests from the list."

She laughed, a low sexy sound. "I have a feeling that you could talk your way out of any difficult situation."

He grinned at her. "Why aren't you married?" he

asked. "You're gorgeous and bright. Even if you aren't particularly interested in being married, why don't you have a boyfriend? Why has it been a year since you've been with anyone?"

The sparkle in her eyes dimmed. "I did have a man I was seeing for a while, although not here in town. I was in Florida on assignment and met Todd. We dated for almost three months, then my assignment ended, and that ended our relationship."

He had a feeling there was more to the story than what she'd told him. But he didn't want to know about her heartaches. He didn't want that kind of emotional intimacy with anyone.

"What about you? Any near misses when it comes to matrimony?" she asked.

"Not even close," he replied. "I make sure the women I date understand that I'm not interested in marriage or long-term commitments of any kind." He recognized that his words were not only the truth, but also meant as a reminder to her.

"Not the marrying kind, huh. Neither am I," she said. She stifled a yawn. "And now it's time for me to sneak back to my own room."

For just a brief moment he wanted to tighten his arms around her and keep her from leaving. It might have been nice to wake up to the morning dawn with Meredith in his arms.

The quicksilver desire for that irritated him, and he immediately released her. "Good night," he said before she'd even placed her feet on the floor.

He watched as she got up, her sleek body tempting him for another go round. Thankfully it took her only a minute to pull the nightshirt over her head and step into the bikini panties.

"Good night, Chase," she said softly, then disappeared out of the room.

He immediately turned off the bedside lamp and shoved away that momentary whim of holding her through the night. He'd just closed his eyes when she screamed.

Chapter 7

The scream clawed up her throat and released itself, piercing the silence of the night as she saw the face pressed against her bedroom window. The face was there only a moment, then gone.

Chase burst into her room, a gun in his hand and his eyes narrowed with dangerous intent. "What's wrong?" Urgency deepened his voice.

Meredith pointed at her window. "Somebody was there...looking in. There was a face." She shuddered, fear whipping through her like a bitter winter wind.

At that moment Kathy and Smokey both appeared, Smokey holding a shotgun and Kathy clutching a small revolver. "What's going on?"

Kathy asked. With her free hand she clutched her robe more tightly around her.

"For God's sake put that pea shooter away before you hurt somebody," Smokey exclaimed to Kathy, obviously surprised that she had a gun. He turned his attention to Meredith. "What's wrong?"

Once again Meredith explained that she'd seen somebody at the window. "I'll go check it out," Smokey said.

"I'll come with you," Chase said.

As the two men left the room, Kathy placed an arm around Meredith. "Come on, honey, let's go wait in the kitchen."

Kathy dropped the revolver into the deep pocket of her robe as she and Meredith left the bedroom and walked down the hallway to the kitchen.

It was just a Peeping Tom, Meredith told herself. There was no reason to feel such fear. She was over-reacting and yet no amount of rationalization seemed to be able to banish the fear that chilled her to the bone and twisted her stomach into knots.

Kathy pointed her toward a kitchen chair, then set about making them each a cup of tea. Meredith sank down at the table, grateful for the solid chair beneath her as her legs trembled uncontrollably.

"Did you recognize the person?" Kathy asked as she placed tea bags into the two cups.

Meredith shook her head. "It all happened so fast. I couldn't tell you whether it was a familiar face or not, whether it was blue eyes or brown that

I saw peering in." She wrapped her arms around herself in an attempt to get warm. "I should have paid more attention, but I was so shocked, then I screamed and the face disappeared."

How long had the person been there? Had he watched her change from her clothes into her night-shirt? Had he watched her rub the scented cream on her body in preparation of going to Chase's room? The very thought made her ill. Her skin wanted to crawl right off her body.

Kathy added boiling water from the microwave to the cups, then set one of them in front of Meredith. "Drink up. There's nothing better than hot tea to take the chill out of you."

Meredith dunked her tea bag several times, then placed it on the saucer and added a spoonful of sugar to the cup. She wrapped her hands around it, welcoming the warmth. "I know I'm overreacting, but I feel so creeped out."

"That's not overreaction. That's normal," Kathy replied. "Somebody violated your personal space. Chase insisted a couple years ago that I get a gun and learn how to use it. There are too many creeps in the world these days."

Meredith took a sip of the hot tea, the liquid effectively warming the cold knot in her stomach. "I wish I hadn't screamed. I should have pretended I didn't see him then left the room and run outside to confront him."

Kathy reached out and patted one of Meredith's

hands. "Don't beat yourself up. You reacted on instinct. Maybe it's your secret admirer."

"If you're trying to make me feel better it isn't working," Meredith said dryly.

"I'm not trying to make you feel better. It just makes sense that maybe the person who sent you the roses was the person who peeked in your window."

"What kind of a man does things like that?" Meredith asked. It was a rhetorical question.

At that moment Chase and Smokey came into the kitchen. "Whoever it was, is gone now," Chase said. He'd managed to pull on a pair of jeans but was bare-chested. In the light of the kitchen the scars on his chest stood out.

"We checked all around the house and the immediate area surrounding it," Smokey said. "Who knows in what direction he ran when you screamed. It was probably just some kid looking for a cheap thrill."

Meredith knew he said these words to reassure her and she smiled at him. "Go back to bed, Smokey. I'm sorry for getting you up."

"From now on pull your shades at night," he said. "No sense in giving anyone a free peep show." With these words he ambled out of the kitchen.

Kathy got up from her chair. "I'm heading back to bed, too. When you get to be my age, you need all the beauty sleep you can get." She paused at the doorway. "Are you sure you're okay?"

Meredith nodded. "I'm fine. Thanks, Kathy."

Chase remained standing next to the counter after

Kathy left. "Are you really okay?" he asked. "Do you want to call Sheriff Ramsey and make a report?"

"No, there's not much he can do about it. Besides, these days he's got more important crimes to worry about than some pervert looking into my window. And yes, I'm really okay." She took another sip of her tea. The chill that had gripped her had finally passed. "Go to bed, Chase. I'm fine. I'm just going to finish my tea, then I'm going to bed."

"Are you sure?"

"I'm positive," she replied. Despite the fact that she'd just had a scare, she felt the need to be alone, to try to process everything the night had brought.

"You know where I am if you need me," he said, then left the kitchen.

The idea of going back to his bed and curling up in his arms for the remainder of the night was appealing. Too appealing.

She'd already been shaken up when she'd left his bedroom in the first place. Making love to Chase had been more wonderful than she'd expected. It hadn't just been the passion and intensity coming from him that had shocked her, but it had also been his unexpected tenderness.

That tenderness had found its way into a part of Meredith's heart that had never been touched before. It had frightened her almost as much as the face at the window.

She couldn't allow herself to get involved with Chase on an emotional level. She knew that could only lead to heartbreak. He'd made it very clear that he wasn't looking for any kind of real relationship.

She was nothing more than an appealing convenience, a break in his routine, and that was fine with her. She told herself she had no desire for anything long-term, either. She'd hoped for something like that once, with Todd, and that had ended with nothing but heartache. She didn't hope anymore.

Aware of the kitchen windows being open to anyone's gaze, she quickly finished her tea, carried the cup to the sink, then shut off the light and returned to her bedroom.

Once there the first thing she did was pull the shades on all the windows, making it impossible for anyone to peek in. She tried to visualize that face in her mind, to make sense of it, identify it. But all she got was a blur.

As she got into bed, she realized she hadn't told anyone about the notes she'd received. She wasn't sure what could be served by telling somebody about the notes now. There was certainly no way to discern who might have penned them simply by looking at the block letters.

She had little doubt that whoever had written the love notes had also sent the flowers and peeped into her window. Maybe what she needed to do was hang out more in town and see if she got any creepy vibes from anybody.

Creepy vibes. That's what she'd been feeling for the last month. Until she'd gotten the first note, she'd thought she was just imagining somebody watching her. Now she knew there was a reason for those vibes. Somebody was watching her... wanting her. All she had to do was figure out who and why he didn't just come forward and just ask her for a date.

A secret admirer. It was the stuff that romantic comedy movies were made of, the stuff of young girls' fantasies. But Meredith wasn't a young girl and her life wasn't a movie set.

She forced her eyes closed, seeking sleep to take the disturbing thoughts out of her head. Maybe tomorrow an assignment would come in that would take her away from Cotter Creek and her secret admirer.

She was surprised to see the light of dawn against the drawn window shades when she opened her eyes. She rolled over on her side and gazed at her alarm clock. Just after six. She'd slept through the night without dreams.

Though it had been a late night, she felt rested and ready to take on whatever the day might bring. She showered and dressed in her usual jeans and long-sleeved shirt, then pulled on a lightweight jacket and headed for the kitchen where Smokey and Kathy were already up and drinking coffee.

For a moment they didn't see her standing in the kitchen doorway, and she noticed how they leaned toward each other as they spoke, how there was a quiet intimacy between them that spoke of something more than houseguest and cook.

She had never known Smokey to show any kind of interest in any woman. His life had always been the West family, but there was something in the way he looked at Kathy that made Meredith realize Smokey might want something more from his life.

Her impulse was to warn him that Kathy was an FBI agent and would leave town at the same time Chase left. Guard your heart, she wanted to say to the man who'd helped raise her. Instead she said good morning and stepped into the kitchen.

"Meredith, how are you feeling this morning?" Kathy asked. "Did you sleep all right?"

"Like a baby," she replied. She got herself a cup of coffee, then joined them at the table. "Where's Dad?"

"He got up a little while ago and decided to take an early-morning ride around the property," Smokey said.

"Did we wake him last night with our little excitement," she asked.

Smokey grinned. "You know your dad, even though he won't admit it he's about half-deaf. He didn't hear anything last night."

"Good. I don't want him upset by any of it. I'm sure whoever was looking in the window last night didn't mean any harm." She took a drink of her coffee, then forced a smile to her lips. "I think what I have is a very shy admirer, and hopefully in the next day or two he'll get up his nerve to approach me in a more traditional manner."

"Anymore window peeping and I'm going to kick somebody's butt," Smokey said with his usual gruff flare.

They small talked for a little while longer, then Meredith got up and put her cup in the sink. "I'm going to go say hello to the horses, then take a walk out to the shed in the pasture."

"What in the hell are you going to do out there?" Smokey asked.

"I've been going through some of the boxes that Mom had packed out there."

"Why?" Smokey looked at her as if she'd lost her mind.

"If Meredith has a need to go through her mother's things, then there's nothing wrong with that," Kathy exclaimed. "Believe it or not, Smokey Johnson, some people are sentimental."

Meredith left them arguing about the merits of being sentimental. She walked out the back door, surprised that despite the early hour the sun was already warming the air.

They'd probably pay for these unusually nice days with tons of snow in another month or two. Although she'd played off the peeper from the night before with Smokey and Kathy, her 9 mm was tucked into her waistband beneath the jacket. She wouldn't be unprepared should he decide to show himself.

Again she told herself that she was probably

overreacting, but the idea of being out on the ranch
alone and vulnerable was definitely not appealing.

Her boots whispered through the brown grass as
she headed toward the stables where she spent
several minutes with the horses.

As she left the stables, her gaze shot around the
area, looking for what, she didn't know. There were
plenty of places to hide on the property if somebody
wanted to. Stands of trees were in every direction.
Outbuildings dotted the landscape, making perfect
places for somebody to hide behind.

"Stop it," she muttered with irritation. She
refused to let the benign events of the past couple
of days freak her out. There was no real reason to
believe that any of it was a threat of harm.

The shed loomed in the distance, and she
wondered what had drawn her back here again this
morning. Maybe a dream she hadn't remembered?
Or maybe it had been that in making love with
Chase she'd felt a fierce desire to connect with the
mother she'd never known, a mother she'd love to
ask about men and love and life.

You don't miss what you never have. That's what
people always said, but she mourned the mother
she'd never had.

She unlocked the shed door and stepped inside.
The box she'd looked in the day before was still on
the old sofa. But there were several other boxes
marked with Elizabeth's name.

She put away the one she'd already looked

through, grabbed another one and returned to the sofa where she sat and opened the box.

Once again she found old copies of reviews and playbills and photos. There were fan letters, too. She read each item with interest, lost for a few moments in another life, another time.

The box also contained several of Tanner's report cards from first and second grade, a construction-paper Valentine that read "To Mommy from Zack" and a variety of other items. Because of the mix of family items and Hollywood memorabilia, it was obvious to Meredith this box had been packed away long after her mother had moved to Cotter Creek.

Elizabeth West had given up so much to come here with her husband. She'd left behind a life of luxury and a budding career that most women would have envied.

Once again Meredith stared at a photo of her mother and wondered, *Will that kind of love ever find me?* Would she ever love somebody enough to leave her family, her life here in Cotter Creek?

Unbidden a vision of Chase entered her mind. It would be easy to let him into her heart just a little bit. Seeing the scars on his body had touched a soft core inside her, knowing that they had come from his father had appalled her.

She tried to imagine the little boy he'd been, a boy who had a father who abused him. Even though Meredith had grown up without the benefit of her mother, she'd had the love of both her father and Smokey.

Still, it would be foolish to let Chase into her heart in any small way. That path led to heartache, and she wasn't masochistic enough to want to consciously walk there.

She was about to put all the items back into the box when she realized there were several yellowing folded pieces of paper still in the bottom. She pulled out the first and carefully opened it. Her heart leaped into her throat.

"I've been waiting for you for a very, very long time. You are my destiny."

She stared at the note, and her fingers began to tremble. It was the same. The words and the block lettering were the very same as the notes that had been left on her car windshield.

Scarcely breathing, she set the note aside and reached for another of the papers. The second piece of paper made her heart race so fast she feared she was going to be sick.

"You will be mine forever."

The familiar words shot a trembling through her body. The same. These notes were identical to the ones she had received.

There was one piece of paper left in the box and she stared at it for a long moment, afraid to open it, afraid of what it might say. And yet there was a perverse curiosity that needed to be fed, an overwhelming need to know what might come next.

She picked up the piece of paper. The yellow, brittle paper felt evil in her fingers. She opened it and stared at the block letters.

"It's time."

Horror edged through her as her brain made the logical connection. Somebody had been stalking her mother, and her mother had wound up murdered. That same somebody was stalking Meredith.

Blinded by fear, she whirled around and screamed as her shoulders were grabbed by firm big hands.

Chapter 8

"Whoa," Chase exclaimed as he found himself suddenly looking at the business end of a 9 mm gun. "A little jumpy, are we?"

"What are you doing out here sneaking up on me? I could have shot you." Her voice trembled as she lowered the gun.

"I came out here to tell you if you didn't get back to the house you'd miss breakfast." He frowned, noticing her face was bleached of color. "Are you all right?"

"No. No, I'm not." Her green eyes held fear that forced a flurry of adrenaline through him.

"What's wrong, Meredith?" Her utter stillness

and blanched features caused a rising tension in him. Something had happened, something bad.

"I think my secret admirer is the man who murdered my mother."

She couldn't have surprised him more if she'd told him that she had been impregnated by a marauding alien. "What are you talking about?"

She tucked the gun in the back of her jeans, then grabbed his hand and led him to the sofa. Her ice-cold hand trembled in his. "I was going through a box of my mother's things and I found these." She handed him three pieces of old, yellowed paper.

He read each one, then looked back at her. "Rather troubling, but what does this have to do with you?"

"I got notes." She sank to the sofa and buried her face in her hands.

"You got notes?" He waited for her to continue.

"Just like these. Oh God, he killed my mother and now he wants me."

"Meredith, what are you talking about? What notes did you get? When?" He felt as if he had entered a movie halfway through and now had to play catch-up. Chase didn't like to play catch-up. "Meredith, answer me," he said impatiently.

He set the papers on the arm of the sofa, then sat next to her and pulled her hands away from her face. "What notes?"

As he stared at her she visibly pulled herself together. She straightened her back and some of the color returned to her cheeks. "I got the first one the night of the Fall Festival dance. When I went to my car to go home it was stuck beneath the windshield. 'I've been waiting for you for a very, very long time. You are my destiny.' That's what it said."

He still held on to her hands. It was like holding two ice cubes. "And the next note?"

"I got it yesterday when I was in town. It was on my windshield when I got ready to come home. It said 'You will be mine,' just like the notes that I found in the box. They were written in the same kind of block lettering as the ones I found in my mother's box." Her eyes were dark with a simmering fear. "I haven't gotten the third note yet."

"Why haven't you told me about the notes before now?" He rubbed her hands, trying to warm them up.

She caught her bottom lip with her teeth, for a moment looking more vulnerable than he'd ever seen her. "I thought they were love notes from a secret admirer. I was embarrassed by them. I thought they were a little bit weird, but nothing to be worried about."

"We still don't know that they're anything to worry about," he said. He wanted to take the fear out of her eyes. He needed to reassure her despite the cold, hard knot of apprehension that lay heavy in his chest. "We don't know exactly when your mother got those notes or that they were written by her killer. We don't want to jump to conclusions before we have any facts."

Some of the sharp edge of fear left her eyes but

no warmth crept back into her hands. "You'll probably think I'm crazy, but I've felt it. For the last month I've felt it getting closer to me."

"What? Felt what?"

She licked her lips, as if they were painfully dry. "Evil." The word whispered from her as if forced out against her will.

Meredith West was not a woman given to dramatics. In the brief time he'd known her, she wasn't given to histrionics or exaggeration. The knot in his chest grew a little bigger.

"Come on, let's get out of here." He released her hands and stood. "I think you should go talk to the sheriff. Do you still have the notes you got?"

She nodded and also stood. "They're in a drawer in my bedroom."

He grabbed the notes from the arm of the sofa. "Then we'll take them and these and let the sheriff know what's going on."

"He won't be able to do anything," she said, her voice sounding stronger than it had before. She locked up the shed and they began the walk back to the ranch house.

"That may be true, but it doesn't hurt to have it on record," he replied.

"I don't want anyone to know about this." She shot him a quick glance. "I don't want to worry my father and I sure don't want to stir up my brothers." A hint of stubbornness crept into her voice. "This is my business and I'll handle it."

"There might come a time when you have to tell them," he replied.

"When that time comes I'll deal with it."

"I'll ride into town with you to see the sheriff," he said.

He thought she might protest, but instead she flashed him a look of gratitude. "I would appreciate it."

"Why don't we head into town now and I'll buy you breakfast at the café after we talk to Sheriff Ramsey."

"That sounds like a deal," she replied.

They walked for a few minutes in silence. Although Chase had tried his best to waylay her fears, to convince her that just because she'd gotten the same notes as her mother that didn't mean the same fate awaited her.

Still, even as he'd told her that, told himself that, he couldn't help but wonder what might happen if and when she got the third note.

"It's time."

He didn't know what those words meant, but he had a sick feeling that it wasn't good.

Even though Meredith appreciated how Chase had tried to alleviate her fears, his rational words had done little to do the trick.

When they got back to the house, she asked her father when the boxes had been packed away in the shed. He told her that her mother had packed and sent them to the shed two days before her death.

This information only intensified the bad feeling she had of impending doom. Now, driving into town with Chase in the passenger seat, she mentally repeated all the things Chase had said to her.

There was no reason to believe that the notes had anything to do with her mother's death—except she believed they did. There was no way to know exactly when her mother might have received the notes in relationship to her murder. And yet Meredith felt the connection in her very bones, in her very soul.

Evidence didn't always matter. Sometimes you had to go with your gut instinct, and Meredith's gut instinct was screaming that her mother's murderer now had her in his sights.

"You know it won't help going to Sheriff Ramsey," she said, needing conversation to halt the thoughts whirling around in her head. "There's not much he's going to be able to do about this."

"I know, but I still think it's a good idea to make a report. Besides, who knows what he might be able to find out." He was silent for a moment then continued, "You know, maybe your mother had a secret admirer. Maybe it's the same person as your secret admirer, but that doesn't mean he's a killer."

She flashed him a quick glance. "Do you really believe that?"

"I'm not sure what to believe at this point," he admitted. "But I think it would be a mistake to jump to any conclusions. Right now all we know for sure is that it looks like a person who wrote notes to your mother is also writing notes to you."

She parked her car in front of the sheriff's office and grabbed the two plastic bags on the seat between them. One contained the notes she had found in her mother's box. The other contained the ones she'd received. "Let's get this over with," she said and got out of the car.

Molly Richmond, the dispatcher and reception-ist, greeted them and told them Sheriff Ramsey was in his office. She led them down the hallway to his inner sanctum.

He rose in surprise as Meredith and Chase walked in. "Meredith…Mr. McCall, what brings you here?" He gestured them into the two chairs in front of his desk and shut the back door that he'd apparently had open to allow in some fresh air.

Chase remained silent as Meredith explained to Sheriff Ramsey about the notes she'd received, the roses and the notes she'd found in the box of her mother's things.

When she'd finished, the sheriff leaned back in his chair, a deep frown cutting across his broad forehead. "I'll send those notes to the lab in Oklahoma City and see if they can pull anything off them."

"My fingerprints will be all over them," she said.

"And so will mine." Chase grimaced, as if irri-tated with himself for touching the notes.

"Then we'll see if the lab can get anyone else's

off them, although I've got to tell you I don't have much hope. If what you think is true, if the person who wrote those notes is the same person who killed your mom, then he's been smart enough to have eluded everyone for twenty-five years. I figure he's smart enough not to leave behind any fingerprints."

"Of course, there's no way of knowing if the person who wrote these notes is the same person who might have killed Elizabeth," Chase said. "We just thought it was important to make a report of what we found and about the notes Meredith has been receiving."

"Absolutely," Sheriff Ramsey agreed. He looked at Meredith for a long moment, his expression soft. "I was the one who found your mom that night. I was a young deputy and I saw her car off at the side of the road and went to investigate."

All his features tightened and he shook his head. "I'll never forget it. There were sacks of groceries in the back of the car, and she was laid out on the ground like she was sleeping." He shook his head again as if to rid his brain of a bad memory. "We investigated her death vigorously at the time." He looked at Chase. "Did she show you the file?"

"Yeah, I looked it over. It looked to me like you all did everything possible to investigate the crime."

"We did. The town was in an uproar. She was well liked and it was such a tragedy." He looked down at the top of his desk for a minute, then looked back at Meredith. "It's possible whoever wrote those notes means no harm at all, but my recommendation to you is for you to be aware of your surroundings and just be careful."

Meredith nodded, oddly disappointed. She wasn't sure what she had expected. Perhaps she'd hoped that Sheriff Ramsey would look at the handwritten notes and exclaim that he knew who had written them. Of course that was crazy because the block letters could have been written by anybody.

"Well, that was a wasted effort," she said a few minutes later as they left the office.

"Not necessarily," Chase replied. "Who knows what Ramsey might stumble on, now that he knows what's going on and about the notes."

She started toward her car, but he grabbed her by the elbow. "Oh no, we aren't going back to the ranch yet," he said. "I already missed one breakfast, and part of the deal was that we'd stop in at the sheriff's office, then have breakfast at the café."

She'd thought she just wanted to go home, but maybe the clatter of noise and friendly conversation in the café would take her mind off things.

"Breakfast sounds good," she agreed.

As they headed across the street toward the café she once again felt as if somebody was watching her. The morning sun cast shadows between buildings and in the overhangs of storefronts, and she wondered if somebody was hiding in one of those shadows watching her progress, wanting her for some sick reason.

She was grateful to get inside the café where the morning crowd was noisy and there were no shadows. She and Chase grabbed a booth toward the back, both of them moving to slide into the booth so they faced the door.

He pointed her to the opposite side, as if he understood her need to face out and watch for danger. "I'm on duty. You sit and relax."

Relax. Would she ever be relaxed again? At the moment every muscle in her body ached with stress, every nerve ending felt as if it was exposed.

"Talk to me, Chase," she said after the waitress had taken their orders and they each had a cup of coffee in front of them.

"What do you want to talk about?"

"Anything. Everything," she exclaimed with a hint of desperation. "I just want you to take my mind off all of this."

His eyes glimmered with a touch of humor. "We could talk about sex. It's been my experience that when it's on my mind, I find it hard to think about much of anything else."

She laughed, surprised that she was still capable of amusement. "You're such a man," she replied.

He grinned. "I'll take that as a compliment."

"You can also take it that I don't want to talk about sex," she replied. She wished he'd never mentioned it, because now her head filled with memories of making love with him. "Tell me about your life in Kansas City."

"There's not a lot to tell," he replied. "I live in a ranch house that I bought two years ago, but I spend most of my time working. In the small amount of leisure time I have, I like to ride my bike and do yard work. It's a pretty normal life."

"What made you decide to become a cop?"

He leaned back in the booth, and his hand reached up to touch the faint white scar that bisected his eyebrow. "When I was sixteen I got up one morning and went to school as usual, but while I was at school I remembered that it was my dad's payday."

He paused and took a drink of his coffee, and any hint of a smile that had been on his face was gone. His eyes took on a darker hue and she knew his memories were bad ones.

"Paydays weren't good?" she asked.

"They were hell. It was my dad's usual habit on paydays to stop after work at one of the local casinos. He'd drink and gamble away most of the check, then come home in the foulest mood imaginable."

"And you were his favorite scapegoat."

He smiled then, a tight expression that did nothing to lighten the darkness of his eyes. "You've got it. Anyway, the longer I thought about it that particular day, the sicker I got. I was tired, sick and tired of him and my life. I skipped the rest of the school day and went home. I packed a bag, took whatever cash I could find around the house, then split for good. I wasn't going to take one more beating. I wasn't going to listen to one more of his drunken apologies or empty promises."

"Where did you go?" She realized she wanted to know everything about him. She knew where he liked to be touched when making love, she knew that a kiss in the hollow of his throat made him groan.

But she wanted to know what kind of man he was, what choices he'd had to make in his life that had formed Chase McCall.

"My dad and I lived in St. Louis and all I knew was that I needed to get out of there. I wanted to go somewhere where he'd never find me and wouldn't be able to force me to come back home. I had enough money for a bus ticket to Kansas City and that's where I went."

Meredith tried to imagine what it had been like for a sixteen-year-old to strike out on his own for a different city, a life alone. "You must have been terrified."

This time his smile did reach his eyes. "Nah, I was too stupid to be terrified. Anything had to be better than the life I'd been living, even life on the streets."

The conversation halted as the waitress appeared with their orders. When she left again Chase continued. "Anyway, I lived on the streets for about two months, sleeping under highway overpasses, eating whatever I could scrounge. I met a lot of people, sad homeless men without hope, drug addicts without a future. I realized that if I didn't do something positive with my life I was going to end up either dead or in jail. I got a job sweeping floors and stocking for a man who ran a little food mart. He let me sleep on a cot in the storeroom and I got my GED. Student loans and financial aid helped me get a bachelor's degree, then I was accepted into the police academy and the rest is history."

"What happened to your father? Did you ever see him again?"

"Two years ago I got word that he was ill so I went back to St. Louis to see him. He was still angry with me for abandoning him. He told me all he'd ever done was love me and I'd run out on him." Chase shook his head and emitted a humorless laugh. "He'd either rewritten history or didn't even remember the abuse. Anyway, he died not long after."

"That's sad," she said. She wanted to reach out and touch his hand. She wanted to pull him into her arms and somehow comfort the child he had been.

He shrugged. "It's the past. They say what doesn't kill you makes you strong."

She wondered if perhaps he hadn't been made too strong? He seemed to be a man who needed nobody. He'd made it clear he wasn't willing to invite anyone into his life, into his heart for any extended period of time. Not that she cared. Not that she wanted to be in his life, she told herself.

"Now are you ready to talk about sex?" he asked, the twinkle back in his eyes.

She laughed and sat back in the booth and wondered when she'd begun to like this man. Certainly she had wanted him, but the warmth that flooded through her now had nothing to do with physical desire.

It had everything to do with the fact that she liked being with him, she liked the way his brain worked and the unexpected humor that transformed his features from something slightly dangerous to something decidedly wonderful.

"Thank you," she said. She pushed away her empty plate.

"For what?"

"For making me forget for a few minutes. For letting me enjoy my breakfast without thinking about anything but you."

"Then we're even because I haven't been able to think of anything but you since last night."

She felt as if the confines of the café got smaller as his gaze lingered on her lips. "You're a dangerous man, Chase McCall," she said softly.

He laughed, low and deep, the sound rumbling inside her. "You ready to get out of here?" he asked.

She nodded and together they got up from the booth. It was only as they arrived at her car and she'd checked the windshield for a note that she realized it was now a waiting game.

Sooner or later she knew she'd get a third note. "It's time." She had no idea what those two words meant, but she definitely had a feeling it wasn't good.

Chapter 9

Chase sat on the bench next to Sam Rhenquist and pulled the collar of his jacket up around his neck. Over the past two days the warm weather had fled and cold Northern air had swooped south to settle in.

"You sit out here all year long?" Chase asked the old man.

"Unless it's raining," Sam replied. "I dozed off one day last year during a snowfall. Didn't wake up until old Mrs. Johnson came by and thought I was dead. She screamed so loud it about broke my eardrums."

Chase smiled and stole a glance at his watch. Meredith was having lunch with Savannah, and he'd ridden into town with her. In fact, over the past two days he'd been right at her side unless she was inside the house.

"She won't be out for another hour or so," Sam said, apparently noticing the glance at the watch. "When those two women get to gabbing it's always a two-hour lunch."

"Are you married, Sam?"

"Was married for forty-two years. Abby passed away on a warm summer night. She rubbed my back until I fell asleep, then died peaceful without making a sound."

"Must be tough to find yourself alone after all those years," Chase said.

Sam smiled. "I hear her voice in my head all the time. I never think about her being gone. She's with me all the time." He pointed across the street to an old woman with a cane heading into the Curl Palace. "That's old Mrs. Crondale. She lost her husband two years ago and her grief has made her one of the most miserable, bitter women in town. She gets her hair done once a week then heads to the café to get a cup of soup and under-tips the waitress."

Once again Chase was struck by how much the old man knew about the comings and goings of the people. "Sam, I'm going ask you straight out. You know something about the deaths of those ranchers?"

Sam gazed across the street, his weatherworn face not changing expression. "I know a lot of things about most of the people of Cotter Creek, some things I'm sure they'd rather nobody else knew. But I don't know who killed those men."

"You're a smart man, Sam. Surely you've got some idea," Chase pressed.

Sam turned back and looked Chase square in the eyes. "I'm smart enough to know better than to talk to a man who isn't what he's pretending to be."

Surprise jolted through Chase. "What are you talking about?"

Sam gave him a look of disgust. "You aren't here for a little vacation. When folks get a chance to go on vacation they sure as hell don't choose to come to Cotter Creek. Besides, you got a look about you that tells me you're here for another reason."

Chase was silent for a long moment, considering his options. "I trust you, Sam. I trust you to be a man who can keep his mouth shut when it's important. I'm FBI."

Sam nodded. "I figured as much." He sat forward and reached for a cup of coffee on the ground next to the bench. The drink was in a to-go cup from the café.

Chase hoped like hell that he hadn't made a mistake in confiding in Sam. It wasn't exactly a great thing to be undercover and then tell people about it. But his instincts told him he could trust the old man.

"I saw Sheila meet with a stranger one night," Sam said. He took a sip of his coffee, then continued. "It was right about the time that the Nesmith place was sold. I figure the man I saw her with was this Joe Black that everyone is talking about, the man who owns MoTwin."

Chase nodded. "We know Black came into town several times over the course of the last year to sign contracts on behalf of the MoTwin Corporation."

"What I never understood was what business he might have over at the newspaper office."

Every nerve in Chase's body electrified. "You saw Joe Black go to the newspaper office?"

Sam nodded. "After hours. Ray Buchannan met him at the door and they were inside together for about an hour."

"Have you told anyone else about this?" Chase's mind whirled. He knew from Meredith that Raymond Buchannan had just made Savannah an offer on the paper. He had plans to get out of town. Now his retirement plans took on a different perspective.

"I didn't know who to tell," Sam said. "Didn't know who to trust and I damn sure didn't want to be seen consorting with those suited fools you all sent to town."

"Thank you for trusting me." Chase knew he needed to call the two agents as soon as possible and give them this lead. Hopefully it would result in the end of this assignment and he could leave Cotter Creek far behind.

Or could he? Even though every day he felt the need to leave, he knew he couldn't walk away knowing that Meredith might be in danger. There had been no more flower deliveries, no more notes, but Chase felt as if they were in a holding pattern and waiting to see what happened next.

He glanced over to where her car was parked. There was no way she'd get a note on her windshield today without him seeing who put it there.

Maybe there won't be another note, he thought. Maybe whoever had sent them was finished, momentarily obsessed with Meredith as they might have been with her mother. Obsession was rarely good. And no matter how he tried to twist his mind to convince himself there was no danger, he wasn't quite successful.

At that moment Meredith and Savannah walked out of the café. Meredith's gaze found him, and the smile that lit her features caused a flutter of crazy regret in his gut.

If the lead that Sam had just given him led to solving the land-scheme crimes, then Chase's work here would be done. What shocked him was the realization that he wasn't ready to say goodbye to Meredith.

He stood to wait for her as she said goodbye to Savannah, who then disappeared into the newspaper office. As Meredith walked toward him, the familiar heat of a simmering desire stoked through him. It had been with him for the past two days as he'd scarcely let her out of his sight.

The problem was he didn't know whether to act on it or ignore it. She was getting to him in ways no woman had ever gotten to him before. Even though he'd known her less than two full weeks, he felt as if he'd known her for half a lifetime. He was comfortable in her presence. Aside from the desire he felt for her, he liked the way she thought, admired her and enjoyed the sound of her laughter.

He wanted to run from her because she stirred in him a hunger for something more than he'd had in his life. She drew him to her, and he felt the need to fight like hell to keep some sort of distance.

Kathy certainly hadn't been overthrilled at the news that he'd told Meredith who they really were and exactly why they were here. "Too close," she'd warned him. "You're getting too close."

"Hi," Meredith said as she stopped in front of him. "Good afternoon, Mr. Rhenquist."

"What's good about it?" he asked with his usual scowl.

She smiled, obviously not bothered by his attitude. "What's good about it? I just had a wonderful lunch with my best friend. Even though the wind is cold, the sun is shining and today's meat loaf at the café was the best I've ever tasted."

"You better not let Smokey hear you say that," Rhenquist replied. "That man takes great pride in his cooking skills."

"You're right," she said with a laugh. "The meat loaf will be our little secret." She looked at Chase. "You ready?"

He nodded and with a goodbye to Sam, he and Meredith headed for her car. It was obvious her lunch with Savannah had been pleasant. Her mood was light, and he felt his mood responding likewise.

"It must have been a good lunch," he said as they got into the car. "You look like you had a good time."

She started the engine, a smile curving her lush lips. "I always have a good time with Savannah. She's so bright and funny." A faint frown creased her forehead. "You know she had terrible parents, too. Her mother basically told her she was ugly and no man would ever fall in love with her, and her dad simply ignored her."

"That's too bad," he said, as always finding it hard to concentrate on anything but the scent of her, which always reminded him of their night together.

"She and Joshua met when they were both investigating the death of Charlie Summit. He was an old man who lived on the edge of town, and he was killed for his land." She flashed him a quick glance. "But you probably know about that."

"I do." Before his arrival in Cotter Creek, Chase had read all the files concerning all the deaths.

"Anyway, the big news is not only did Savannah sign the papers to make the newspaper hers, but she and Joshua set a date for their wedding. Isn't that terrific?"

"It's great. My big news is that Sam told me that Joe Black had business with Raymond Buchannan late one night after newspaper hours."

She looked at him with surprise, then quickly focused her attention back on the road. "Wow. So, you think maybe Buchannan is behind it all?"

"I'm not sure what to think, but he definitely just rose to the top of the suspect list as far as I'm concerned. In fact, when I get back to the ranch I need to call Wallace and Tompkins and let them know what Sam told me."

She shook her head, the dark strands beckoning him to touch them. "Raymond Buchannan. I just can't believe it. He's been a lifelong resident here. Why on earth would he betray his town, his friends and neighbors?"

"Whoever orchestrated this stood to gain tons of money," he replied. "Love or money, those seem to be at the crux of almost every crime committed."

For a few minutes they rode in silence. Chase stared out the window, fighting the wealth of need that pressed inside him. The need to hold her in his arms once again, the need to taste her mouth one more time.

"You don't have to do this you know," she finally said.

"Do what?" He looked at her curiously.

"You don't have to go everywhere with me. You don't have to be with me every minute that I'm away from the house. I know how to take care of myself. I'm a professional bodyguard."

He looked at her, taking in the soft curve of her jaw, the long lashes that framed her impossibly green eyes. "It's my professional opinion that the bodyguard needs a bodyguard."

She flashed those gorgeous eyes his direction once again. "I think maybe we're both overreacting to the notes. I mean, yes, it's creepy that somebody wrote notes to my mother and apparently is now writing them to me. But that doesn't mean it was the person who killed her."

"I'm aware of that," he replied. "But I'm also aware that we can't know right now that the note writer wasn't responsible for your mother's death. I'd feel better if we could learn the identity of the person who wrote those notes. It's possible he's nothing more than a harmless eccentric who had a crush on your mother years ago and now has a crush on you."

"That would mean he's probably old," she replied. She flashed him a smile that didn't quite lift the shadows from her eyes. "If he's old, then I could probably take him in a brawl."

"There's no guarantee he's that old," Chase replied. "Maybe he was just a teenager when he got a crush on your mother. That would mean he might be as young as forty."

"Buck Harmon's age," she replied thoughtfully.

"Or a dozen other men in town."

She pulled her car up in front of the house and turned off the engine. "For the last month or so I've had the feeling of somebody watching me." She turned in the seat to look at him. "You know that prickly sensation you get on the back of your neck when you feel like you're being watched."

"But you haven't seen anyone suspicious? Don't have a clue who might be watching you?"

She shook her head. "Believe me, if I did I'd

confront them." She paused a moment, her expression thoughtful. "So, if this lead about Raymond Buchannan pans out, then you'll probably be leaving soon."

"We'll see how things play out," he replied. He got out of the car then, needing distance, fighting the ever-present desire for something he couldn't quite define, something that scared the hell out of him.

He managed to keep his distance from her for the remainder of the day. He made the phone call to Agent Wallace, then spent the afternoon chatting with Red about ranch life, his children and the family business.

Even while he talked to Red, he was always conscious of where Meredith was in the house. It was as if he had a built-in radar where she was concerned. She spent most of the afternoon in the kitchen with Smokey and Kathy, then went to her room.

He didn't see her again until dinner. Tanner and Anna arrived to share the meal, Anna glowing with happiness as she stroked the bulge of her pregnant stomach.

As they ate, Smokey and Kathy argued about the right way to make brisket, Tanner and Anna talked about their plans for their growing family and Chase found himself unable to take his attention off Meredith.

Instead of her usual jeans and flannel shirt, she'd changed for dinner into a pair of slim black slacks and a deep-burgundy blouse that did amazing things to her creamy complexion. She made it damn hard for him to concentrate on the meal.

It was after supper and after Tanner and Anna had left when Meredith said she was headed out to the barn to check on the horses.

Chase grabbed his jacket and fell into step with her. "I doubt I need bodyguard protection in my own stables," she said as they walked toward the wooden structure in the distance. "Besides, I have my gun." She moved the side of her jacket to show the weapon stuffed into her waistband.

"Armed women always turn me on," he said teasingly.

"I think probably breathing women turn you on," she retorted with a laugh.

"That's not true," he protested. "You make me sound like a helpless womanizer and I'm not."

"I know you aren't. I was just teasing." She fell silent as they reached the stables.

He sat on a bale of hay and watched as she went from stall to stall. She seemed softer here, oddly vulnerable as she greeted the horses with a whispered voice and a stroke on the head. He could almost see the tension rolling off her shoulders, disappearing from her facial features.

It was as if the world shrank to nothing bigger than the interior of the stable with the scent of hay and horse and leather, and he knew by her posture and her facial expression that this had always been a safe place for her.

When she was finished telling each of the animals good-night, she joined him on the bale of hay, as if reluctant to go directly back to the house.

Instantly he was aware of her scent, that arousing smell of jasmine. "You like it out here, don't you."

She smiled. "This was always my place. You can't imagine how difficult it was to grow up with five brothers who loved nothing better in the world than to torment and tease me. This was always where I'd run if I needed to cry or I needed to cuss."

He laughed and tried to imagine her as a child. "But surely you had girlfriends who you could talk to, bond with."

Her smile turned rueful. "That's the other problem with having five gorgeous brothers. Most of the girls who wanted to be my best friend really just wanted to hang out here and be around my brothers."

"It sounds lonely."

She frowned thoughtfully, then turned to look at him. "I know you've said you have no intention of getting married or anything like that, but don't you ever get lonely, Chase?"

He wanted to answer her with a resounding no, but the very question itself illuminated the loneliness he'd struggled with for a very long time. And it irritated him, that somehow in the past two weeks at the West ranch, she'd made him feel that loneliness again.

"Never," he replied curtly. He stood. "We should probably get back to the house. It's getting dark."

He didn't look at her, was afraid that if he did she might see the lie in his eyes, might know the depth of loneliness that had always been with him.

Chapter 10

That night Meredith lay in bed fighting against a restlessness she'd never known before, and she suspected the restlessness had a name and its name was Chase.

It had been days since he'd touched her, since he'd kissed her, and there was a burn of want in the pit of her stomach. There was no denying the tension that existed between them every moment that they were together. But he'd made no move to act on it.

And that's good, she told herself as she rolled over on her back and stared up at the ceiling where the moonlight danced with faint silver hues. It was good because she was falling in love with Chase McCall.

She hadn't planned it; she didn't even want it, but there it was. He'd gotten to her with his sharp blue eyes and edge of arrogant confidence. He'd touched her with his easy laughter and sexy flirting. But more than anything, he'd crawled directly into her heart when she'd seen a flash of his wounded soul.

She wasn't a rescuer, knew that there was no way to take away the pain of his past. But, God help her, she wished she could be part of his future.

It wouldn't be long before he and Kathy would pack their bags and leave Cotter Creek behind. Meredith had a feeling Smokey would miss Kathy desperately. She'd never seen him so animated, so ready with a smile as he was when Kathy was around.

There would be hearts needing healing when they left. And they would heal…eventually. She squeezed her eyes closed, willing away thoughts of Chase.

Instead she focused on the question of who might be her secret admirer. He could be as young as forty or as old as her father. That certainly didn't lessen the list of potential suspects, rather it pointed a finger to almost any man in Cotter Creek.

The notes held the quality of obsession rather than love. If she were to guess, the person had been obsessed with her mother, and because Meredith was the spitting image of her mother, she'd now garnered the attention of the same person.

So what did he want from her? Why hadn't he made himself known yet? Was it possible that he'd identified himself to her mother, and Elizabeth had rebuffed him? Had that been the end of it, or was he the man who had flagged Elizabeth down on the side of the road and strangled the life out of her?

Meredith wasn't even sure if her fear was warranted. But warranted or not, she couldn't help the cold chill that gripped her heart each time she thought of those notes. She couldn't help the instincts that screamed that something bad was going to happen.

A soft knock fell on her door. She reached out to turn on the nightstand lamp, then slid out of bed and to her bedroom door. She opened it an inch to see Chase.

"I lied," he said softly. "I do get lonely. I'm lonely right now."

She knew she had two choices. She could either open the door all the way and let him in or she could tell him to go back to bed and shut the door.

If she let him in, there was no question that they would make love again. There was no question that her feelings for him would only intensify. But if she sent him back to his room she had a feeling she would regret it for the rest of her life.

She opened the door wider and once he was in her room she closed it behind him. He stood for a long moment, his gaze searching hers as if seeking the answer to a question he hadn't voiced.

Taking his hand, she led him to her bed. He laid the condom he'd brought with him on the nightstand, then took off his boxers and slid beneath her sheets.

He was going to break her heart, this man with passion in his eyes. He was going to break her heart and there was nothing she could do about it.

With a sense of both resignation and sweet anticipation, she pulled off her nightgown and joined him in the bed. He reached for her and she went willingly into his arms even knowing that there was a piece of her heart she would never be able to claim back from him.

His kiss was achingly tender, his lips soft against hers. It was impossible for her to think when she was in his arms, impossible to do anything but feel.

He seemed to be in no hurry but rather moved with a languid sensuality, as if he recognized they had all the hours of the long night ahead of them.

As he caressed her breasts first with his hands, then with his mouth, unexpected tears pressed hot at her eyes. This would be the last time she'd feel his touch, taste his mouth. As much as she cared about him, she wouldn't, couldn't do this again.

This knowledge made each kiss, every touch more intense and tinged with a bittersweet element. They didn't say a word, but no words were necessary as the kisses grew deeper and the caresses hotter and more intimate.

He knew just where to touch and kiss her to evoke the most intense response…her inner thigh, the skin just behind her ear, the back of her knees.

And she responded in kind, finding the places on

his body that produced a deep moan and tightened all his muscles and made him hoarsely whisper her name.

When they were both gasping and aching with need, it was she who put the condom on him, she who urged him to move over her and take her.

She wanted to be lost in him, and as he stroked deeply into her she *was* lost. She gave him everything—her passion, her tenderness and her heart. And at least while they made love she felt as if she had his in return.

Afterward she expected him to get up and creep back to his own room, but he didn't. He went to the bathroom, then returned and got back beneath her sheets.

The lamp that she had turned on when she'd heard the knock on her door had remained on during their lovemaking. He now reached over her to turn it off, then gathered her into his arms.

His heartbeat was strong and steady against hers and she nuzzled her head into his shoulder, wishing for things that would never be, wanting something different than she knew the future contained.

But she couldn't change anything that might come. All she could do was grasp with both hands the moment happening right now.

"I spent a lot of years being lonely," he said softly as one of his hands stroked the length of her hair. "I sometimes think I invented lonely."

His words pierced through her, and once again she wished she could go back in time and fix the pain and isolation he'd felt as a child. As the only girl in the West family, she'd certainly at times felt isolated and alone, but she'd always known that she had a houseful of people who loved her, people who would never really hurt her.

"Was there nobody you could talk to? Nobody to tell about your dad's abusiveness?"

He sighed. "Looking back now there were probably people I could have told. Maybe a teacher or a neighbor. But at the time it never occurred to me. And even if it had, I think I would have been too afraid to tell. Besides, as crazy as it sounds, there was a part of me that was fiercely protective of my dad."

She knew he'd gifted her with a piece of himself that he'd probably never shared before and she was honored by that.

"Anyway," he continued. "I learned to live with the loneliness. It's been a part of my life for so long I'm not sure I'd feel right without it."

She tightened her arms around him, wanting to memorize the feel of his body next to hers, the scent of his skin that filled her head. She closed her eyes as she matched her breathing to his.

For the first time in her life she felt as if she belonged where she was, in Chase McCall's arms. And all too quickly he'd be out of her life.

He leaned against the side of the house, fighting the rage that swept through him. His tight chest made it hard to breathe, and he fisted his hands into balls at his side.

He'd come here hoping to get a glimpse of Meredith, just a quick peek of her to feed him, to sustain him until he could make her his forever. Her shades had been drawn but one of them wasn't completely down and gave him a tiny peephole into her room.

He'd looked in and had been shocked as he saw Meredith and Chase McCall moving intimately together beneath the sheets on the bed.

He now squeezed his eyes tightly closed as if he could banish the image.

It was his fault…Chase McCall. He'd seduced her, just like Red West had seduced the sweet Elizabeth so many years ago.

He'd pay. Chase McCall would pay. There was no way anyone was getting in the way this time, especially not some big-city boy with his sweet-talk and charm.

He stole away from the house the way he had come, melting into the shadows of the night.

Chase awoke with the dawn, for a moment disoriented as he gazed at his surroundings. Then he remembered he was in Meredith's room. He turned his head to see her curled up on her side facing him, her features relaxed with sleep.

He watched her for a long moment, taking in the strong features that worked together to create beauty. He'd told her more than he'd ever told anyone about himself and his past. Something about her had encouraged trust and confidence.

It was time to leave, time to escape before she got any further into his heart. She drew him toward her with the promise of no more loneliness, with the promise of happiness. But he was scared of that, afraid that eventually that happiness would shatter and he would show himself to be nothing more than his father's son.

He crept out of bed, careful not to wake her, and stole out of the room. As he stepped into the hallway he was shocked to see Kathy, clad only in a long nightgown, sneaking down the hall toward her bedroom. For a moment they stood and stared at each other, then she quickly disappeared into her room.

So, it's like that, Chase thought as he got dressed a few minutes later. He had no doubt that his partner had spent the night in Smokey's room. It would appear that neither of them had been able to withstand the charm of certain members of the West family.

They were all at breakfast when Clay came in and joined them for coffee. "Where's Libby and Gracie?" Meredith asked her brother.

"They had an appointment over at the Curl Palace for hair cut and styles and manicures and pedicures. I figured I'd come and hang out here with dad while my two girls are doing their girl thing."

"I'm glad," Red said with a smile at his son. "I always like it when you boys come to visit."

"What's everyone's plans for the day?" Clay asked and looked around the table.

"Smokey and I are going into town to buy some groceries," Kathy said while Chase looked at Meredith expectantly. Whatever she had planned he wouldn't be far away. He'd told her the truth when he'd said that the bodyguard needed a bodyguard.

"I thought I might do a little riding after breakfast," she said.

"Riding?" Chase frowned. "I hope you're talking about riding in your car."

A faint whisper of a smile curved her lips. "No, I'm talking about getting on my horse. I haven't taken Spooky out for over a week. She needs a good ride. Besides, I figured it was time you got on the back of a good horse."

"Do you ride, Chase?" Clay asked.

"Never in my life," he replied.

"There's almost nothing better than being on the back of a horse on a fall morning," Red said. "Meredith's a fine horsewoman. She'll get you set up and you'll never forget the experience."

"That's what I'm afraid of," he said dryly.

As they finished breakfast, Clay told them about a new advertising campaign his stepdaughter, Gracie, had been offered. "It's a new line of kids' clothes. They're using her for the print ads and then in November we're flying to New York to do a television commercial."

Chase knew that Clay had gone to California to

work as a bodyguard for eight-year-old Gracie who was a successful child star. In the process of caring for the child, he'd fallen in love with Gracie's mother, Libby.

"We're being very selective of what we let her do, but she wanted to do this, and both Libby and I like the people involved," Clay continued.

The conversation remained pleasant for the rest of the meal. When they were finished eating, and Smokey and Kathy were clearing the dishes, Meredith shot him a quick smile. "Go on, cowboy, get a jacket and then it's time to introduce you to a horse."

After he went to his room and she went to hers, they met in the hallway, both wearing jackets for the brisk morning air.

"I can't believe you're going to do this to me," he said as they left the house and headed in the direction of the stables.

"Oh, stop whining, Mr. FBI Agent," she chided teasingly. "If you ride motorcycles, then a horse should be a piece of cake."

"A motorcycle does what you tell it to do because it doesn't have a brain. A horse is more unpredictable." He grinned at her, noting how the morning sunshine sparkled in her hair. "I'll tell you what, you ever come to Kansas City I'll get you on a motorcycle and see how comfortable you feel."

Her smile faltered just a tad. "I may come to Kansas City someday. As much as I love it here I don't see my future here forever."

Her words surprised him. "Really? Why?"

"For a while now I've had a desire to get away from Cotter Creek, find my own place in a city where nobody knows my family."

"What would you do?" He'd never thought that Meredith would have any desire to leave this quaint town or her family.

"I don't know, maybe join a police department or go into private investigation or maybe do something altogether different."

"You know if you ever come to Kansas City and want to apply at the police department I could put in a good word for you."

"Thanks, I appreciate it." She opened the stable door, and they walked in to see a young man brushing down one of the horses. "Good morning, Brian," she greeted.

"Morning." He smiled pleasantly.

"You want to saddle up Sugarpie while I get Spooky?"

"No problem." He led the horse he'd been brushing back into a stall, then disappeared into another stall.

"I'm going to ride a horse named Sugarpie?" Chase followed behind her as she walked toward her own horse. "My masculinity balks at the very thought."

She laughed. "Would you rather I put you on a horse named Thunder or Lightning?"

He pretended to consider it. "Nah, I guess Sugarpie is a good choice for a first ride."

He watched as she got to work saddling up Spooky. They hadn't spoken about last night, but when she'd seen him this morning there had been a secretive smile on her lips and in her eyes that had made him want to take her into his arms once again.

She was the strongest woman he'd ever known, not just in a physical sense, for he'd seen at the dance that she could take care of herself. But she radiated a quiet strength of character that he found incredibly appealing, a strength of character he thought every previous woman in his life had lacked.

She didn't need him. She would be fine when he left. At least that's what he told himself. But there were moments when he saw such vulnerability in her eyes, moments when he thought he saw love for him in those green depths.

He didn't want her to love him. He didn't want to leave here knowing he left behind pain. She'd told him she had no interest in anything long-term, in anything permanent, but something about the way she looked at him, the way she touched him denied her words.

"All set," Brian said as he led a huge chestnut mare toward Chase.

"Perfect timing," Meredith replied, her horse saddled and ready to ride, as well. She led both horses out of the stable and into the corral. "The only thing you have to remember is tug left to go left, tug right to go right and pull up on the reins to stop." She flashed him a reassuring smile. "You won't have any problems. Sugarpie is always willing to please."

He watched her mount her black horse and he couldn't help but admire how good she looked, confident and relaxed, but almost regal.

Although Chase had never been on the back of a horse in his life, he had seen enough western movies to know how to get on one. He placed a foot in the stirrup and swung himself up and into the saddle. "Piece of cake," he said.

"You look good in the saddle, cowboy," she replied, then took off.

Chase nudged his horse in the ribs with his heels and Sugarpie responded, following Meredith at an easy pace. It took him a couple of minutes to adjust to the rhythm and sway, but by the time they hit open pasture he felt as if he was getting the hang of the motion of the animal beneath him.

Red was right. There was nothing quite as magnificent as riding a horse with the brisk morning air whipping through your hair and filling your lungs with the scents of earth and sunshine and horse. Add to that the pleasure of watching Meredith, with her hair tossing and her eyes shining and Chase was a happy man.

The horse seemed to know the usual path that a morning run took and Chase had to do little but hang on as they began to gallop. It was as exhilarating as a motorcycle run and when Meredith finally reined in to slow her horse, he was almost sorry to do the same.

"Not bad for a novice," she said as they came to a halt.

He leaned over and patted Sugarpie's neck. "Thanks. You were right. This is terrific."

"You look like a natural."

"It's a piece of cake."

"Oh, yeah?" Her eyes lit with a hint of challenge. "Then I'll race you to those trees." She pointed in the distance to a thick grove of autumn-colored trees. She took off, Spooky's hooves thundering against the ground.

He laughed and watched her go. He wasn't a fool. He wasn't about to match his horse-riding skills against a woman who'd practically been born on a horse.

He was still laughing when the crack of gunfire split the air. Almost simultaneously he felt a piercing burn in his left side. The pain blackened his sight and he was vaguely aware of casting sideways before the ground rose up and smacked him in the face.

Chapter 11

"Chase!" The scream ripped from Meredith as she reached for her gun, jumped off her horse and hit the ground. She pointed her gun in the direction where she thought the shot had come from but saw no movement in the trees, couldn't find a target to defend them against.

Her heart thundered in her chest with sickening speed as she crawled on all fours across the ground toward Chase. As she reached him he rolled onto his stomach, his gun also out and pointed in the same direction as hers.

"I'm okay," he told her, but she saw the grimace of pain and the sweat that beaded his brow. Fear stole through her.

"Are you hit?" she asked. "Where? Where are you hurt?"

"My left side." His hand holding the gun trembled just a bit, and her fear for him intensified.

"We've got to get you back to the house. Spooky… home!" she shouted. "Home, Spooky."

The horse whinnied as if in response to the command and took off running in the direction they'd come. Sugarpie raced after, leaving Chase and Meredith alone.

"Are you sure that was a good idea?" he asked.

"Hopefully somebody will see them coming home without us and will know we're in trouble." She had scarcely taken her gaze off the stand of trees. "I don't see anyone."

"That doesn't mean nobody is there."

She was heartened by the fact that his voice was still strong, that he didn't appear to be losing consciousness. "Why would somebody want to shoot you? I thought I was the one who might be in danger."

"If I find out one of your overly protective brothers did this, I'm going to be pissed," he said.

She knew it was an attempt at humor, but she couldn't find anything humorous about any of this.

"Maybe somebody found out I'm FBI and think I'm too close to finding out about who is behind the land scheme," he said.

She didn't know how long they remained there, guns pointed, before she heard the familiar sound of a pickup approaching in the distance.

Clay's truck kicked up dust as it sped toward them. Clay drove, Kathy rode shotgun, and Smokey sat in the back, rifle ready. The truck came to a halt a few feet from where they lay and Clay got out.

"What happened?" He reached for Meredith, but she waved him away.

"Help Chase. He's been shot. It came from the trees." She pointed to the grove, and both Smokey and Kathy aimed their weapons in that direction as Clay helped Chase up off the ground.

Meredith cried out as she saw the blood that stained his side. "Get him in the back. We need to go directly to the hospital," she exclaimed.

Clay put him into the pickup, and Meredith and Smokey got in next to him. Within minutes they were out of the pasture and on the road to the hospital.

"Can you tell how bad it is?" Meredith asked. She tried to fight the terror that shivered through her as she saw how pale he was, how much pain he seemed to be in.

He forced a thin smile to his lips. "It hurts like hell, but my heart is still beating and my lungs are still breathing, so I'm guessing it's not life threatening."

Unless he bled to death before they got him to the hospital, or unless some organ had been pierced they weren't aware of. Her head filled with all kinds of terrible things.

Chase reached for her hand and squeezed it. "Don't look so scared. I'm tough. It takes more than a bullet to bring me to my knees."

"I'd just like to know what bastard did this," Smokey said, his expression grim.

"That makes two of us," Chase replied. He closed his eyes, his face more pale by the minute.

When they reached the hospital, two orderlies whisked Chase away, and Meredith sank into a chair in the waiting room, fighting back tears. Kathy sat next to her and took her hand.

"He's tough," she said. "And he was still conscious when we got here. That's a good sign."

Meredith nodded. "We need to call the sheriff. We have to report this."

"Is it possible it was just some sort of freak hunting accident?" Kathy asked. "Maybe somebody target shooting and didn't realize you were in the pasture?"

Meredith frowned thoughtfully. "I suppose anything is possible. Chase thought maybe somebody knows he's FBI and thinks he's getting too close to naming a guilty party." She rubbed her forehead where a headache threatened to split her skin. "Maybe Sam Rhenquist told somebody about Chase." She kept her voice low so that Clay and Smokey couldn't hear their conversation.

"As soon as I know Chase is all right I'll have a little chat with Sam," Kathy said, a steel in her tone that Meredith had never heard before. Meredith had a feeling there were many layers to the cherub-faced, blue-eyed woman seated next to her.

"And I'm going to call Sheriff Ramsey now. I want him here." Meredith took her cell phone and left the waiting room. She stepped outside the small hospital entrance and punched in the number for the sheriff's office. Molly Richmond, the dispatcher answered.

"Molly, this is Meredith West. Is the sheriff in?" Meredith asked.

"He left a while ago. If I was to guess, he was probably heading out for lunch then was going to sit on Highway 10. You know he loves handing out those speeding tickets."

"Can you contact him and tell him to come to the hospital as soon as possible?"

"I should be able to raise him on the radio."

Meredith hung up and for a moment remained standing in the brilliant noon sun. The world she knew had suddenly become a dangerous place. She'd always believed that her home and the surrounding land were a safe haven where nothing bad could happen. Now that sense of security was gone.

The moment that she'd seen Chase slide off his horse and hit the ground, the full extent of her love for him had exploded in her heart.

She'd allowed him in where no man had ever been before and knew when he left Cotter Creek she would never quite be the same again.

She hurried back inside to wait for news of his condition and to wait for the arrival of Sheriff Ramsey. It took two hours before Dr. Carson came out to talk to them.

"The bullet went right through his side. The entrance and exit were both clean and it hit nothing vital, although it did bust a rib. He lost some blood and I'd like to keep him overnight. But, he was damned lucky."

"Can I see him?" Meredith asked.

Dr. Carson hesitated a moment then nodded. "Room 110. He's got some pain medication in him but he's doing just fine."

Meredith turned to her family. "You all might as well go on home. Let Dad know everything is okay."

Clay, Smokey and Kathy left, and Meredith hurried down the hallway, eager to see for herself that he was really okay.

The curtains in room 110 were drawn to guard against the bright sunshine, but a dim light was on above the bed. Chase's eyes were closed, and Meredith crept silently to the chair next to the bed and sank down.

"I don't think I'll be riding a horse again anytime soon," he said without opening his eyes.

"How did you know it was me?"

"I smell your perfume." He opened his eyes. and to Meredith's surprise she began to cry.

She hadn't been aware that she was going to; the tears just brimmed over and a deep sob tore from her. The emotion that she'd kept in check from the moment he'd fallen off his horse until now could no longer be suppressed.

"Hey, don't cry. I'm okay," he said.

"I know, but I can't help it." The words came out between sobs. "I was so scared for you."

There was no way she could explain the horror that had gone through her when she'd heard that shot, then had seen him slide off the back of Sugarpie and hit the ground.

She scrubbed the tears off her cheeks with the backs of her hands and drew a deep breath to get herself under control. "I'm sorry," she exclaimed. "I didn't mean to do that."

He smiled. "Don't apologize. I'm sorry I scared you."

"Maybe my bodyguard needs his own body-guard," she said.

The smile fell from his face. "I'd like to meet the guy who pulled that trigger."

"I called Sheriff Ramsey. He should be here soon, and maybe he'll be able to get to the bottom of it," she replied.

Chase nodded and closed his eyes, and Meredith knew he'd fallen asleep. She remained in the chair, watching over him. She found herself wondering who had watched over him when he'd been little and had been sick? Who had nursed him through the childhood illnesses? The father who had beaten him?

It wasn't pity that stirred in her breast, just a sadness. Even though she hadn't had her mother, she'd had Smokey and Red to nurse her, to stroke her forehead and fix her special treats. She'd been a lucky woman and she hadn't realized just how lucky she'd been until this moment.

Maybe it was time to do as Chase had said, to let

her mother go. She was tilting at windmills, thinking that she could solve a crime that none of the investigating officers had been able to solve at the time it occurred.

Chase was right. Solving the crime wouldn't bring her mother back. Solving the crime wouldn't fill the hole that Elizabeth West's death had left behind. It was time to let it go and get on with her life.

She didn't know how long she sat there watching Chase sleep before Sheriff Ramsey arrived. She stepped out into the hall to talk to him and explain what had happened.

"And you think the shooter was in the trees?" Ramsey asked.

"That's where the shot came from."

"Did Dr. Carson dig out a bullet? If I have a bullet I'll know what kind of gun it came from."

Meredith shook her head. "The bullet made a clean exit."

At that moment Chase called her name, and both Meredith and Sheriff Ramsey went into his room where Ramsey questioned him further.

"I'll need somebody to take me out there and show me exactly where it happened," Sheriff Ramsey said. "Maybe we can find a shell casing or something that the shooter left behind."

"I'll be out of here tomorrow. We'll do it then," Chase said. "I don't want Meredith out there at all."

She started to protest, but then decided not to

argue with a man who'd just been shot and was on pain meds.

Ramsey nodded. "I'll ask some questions around town. It's possible some damn fool was either doing a little target shooting or hunting and didn't realize there were people in the pasture."

He closed his small notebook where he had been taking notes, then tucked it into his breast pocket. "You need a ride home?" he asked Meredith.

"No, thanks. I don't know when I'll be going, and when I do I'll just call somebody at the house to come and get me." She wasn't ready to leave Chase.

"Then I guess I'm finished here. I'll call you if I find out anything." With those words Sheriff Ramsey left.

"I'm not going to hold my breath for a phone call," Chase said once he had gone.

"Kathy said she was going to talk to Rhenquist and see if he told anybody that you were FBI. Maybe she can find out something that will point a finger to a shooter."

"If Kathy finds out who did this before I do, then I pity the guy. If she doesn't kill him outright, she'll make him wish he were dead," he replied, his voice slurring with the edges of impending sleep.

The day passed with Chase sleeping, then awakening to talk for a few minutes with her, then him falling asleep once again.

The nurse came in at regular intervals to take his vitals and administer medication. The phone rang occasionally as members of her family called to see how he was doing.

Night was falling when he encouraged her to go home. "There's nothing you can do here," he said. "I'd feel better if I knew you were at the ranch, sleeping in your own bed instead of here."

"Are you sure? I don't mind staying," she said.

"Please, go," he said gently. "I'll sleep the night through and I'd have more peaceful sleep if I knew you were at the ranch where you belong."

"Okay," she replied. "I'll call and get somebody to pick me up." She made the phone call to the ranch and got her dad, who told her somebody would be there to pick her up in the next twenty minutes or so.

Meredith remained in the room for another ten minutes, then said her goodbye and stepped outside the hospital's main entrance to wait for her ride.

She tried not to think about how tragic this day might have been. She tried to keep her mind off the idea that if the path of that bullet had been an inch or two different, she'd be visiting Chase's body in the morgue rather than in the hospital.

The cool night air seemed to seep beneath her jacket to chill her heart. She wrapped her arms around herself as if to defend against the cold that she knew had little to do with the weather.

A familiar truck pulled into view, although Smokey wasn't behind the wheel. Kathy pulled the truck up to the curb and Meredith got into the passenger side.

"Smokey wanted to come and get you," she said once Meredith was settled in. "I don't know if any of you have noticed it or not, but that damn fool has no business behind a steering wheel after dark."

Meredith smiled. "Believe me, we've noticed, but Smokey is nothing if not bullheaded."

"How's Chase?" she asked as she pulled away from the curb.

"All right. He's been pretty doped up for most of the day, but he seems to be doing fine."

"He's tough," Kathy said. "But sometimes I'm not sure he's as tough as he'd like everyone to think he is."

"Kind of like Smokey," Meredith observed.

Kathy smiled, and in that smile Meredith saw Kathy's affection for Smokey. "Can I tell you a little secret, Meredith?"

"Sure."

"I've spent my whole life focused on the job. I never met a man who I thought I could tolerate for any length of time so I never married, never had children and focused only on work."

She paused a long moment and Meredith waited for her to continue, knowing instinctively that the information Kathy wanted to impart had little to do with her work obsession.

"Then I come out here and meet Smokey Johnson, a cranky old man who thinks he makes better coleslaw than me, and for the first time in my life I feel like a schoolgirl."

"You're in love with Smokey?" Although Meredith had seen the growing relationship between Smokey and Kathy, she'd suspected that Kathy was just playing a role.

"Crazy, huh. The tough-as-nails FBI broad brought to her knees by a cowboy with a bum leg and an attitude as big as Oklahoma." She shook her head and released a small laugh. "And the wonder of it all is that Smokey says he's crazy about me."

"So what happens now for the two of you?" Meredith asked. "It won't be long before the crime that brought you here will be solved."

Kathy nodded. "I'm expecting the case to break wide open in the next day or two. After that I'm returning to Kansas City and retiring, then I'm coming back here and living out the rest of my life with Smokey."

"Kathy, I'm so happy for you and Smokey." Happy tears misted Meredith's vision. "Smokey sacrificed the good years of his life to step in and take care of us."

"Don't let him hear you say that," Kathy replied. "As far as he's concerned sacrifice had nothing to do with it. He loved you all. You were the children he never had. You filled his life with love."

At least somebody was going to get a happy ending, Meredith thought. For she knew in her heart there was no happy ending for her and Chase.

Chase shifted positions on the chair on the porch, wincing as his side throbbed with a dull ache. It had been three days since he'd been released from the hospital.

Thankfully there had been no sign of infection in the wounds, and that morning at an appointment with Dr. Carson, the doctor had been pleased with how quickly Chase was healing.

It wasn't quickly enough for him. He didn't like feeling like an invalid, hated that everyone was waiting on him hand and foot.

The sheriff had been unable to find out who had shot him. Chase hadn't expected any different. He knew how difficult it was to investigate a random shot by an unknown assailant, especially when the shooting occurred in the middle of a pasture. A sweep of the wooded area where the shot had come from had yielded nothing, and unless somebody came forward and confessed, the odds were slim to none that Chase would ever know who was responsible.

Kathy had spoken to Rhenquist, who had been mightily offended that anyone thought he'd broken Chase's confidence. He'd insisted that he'd told nobody about the real reason Chase was in town.

It was now just after ten in the morning. He'd sneaked out here on the porch to have a moment to himself. Meredith had been like a shadow since he'd been home from the hospital. Nurse Nightingale had nothing on Meredith West.

He'd said he was going to his room to lie down. Then while nobody was looking he'd come out here to the porch to sit and think with nobody hovering over him.

Actually, he'd found the hovering rather nice. He knew his convalescence would have been much different in Kansas City. There would have been nobody checking on him, nobody making sure he was okay, because he had never allowed anyone into his life.

And that's the way I like it, he told himself, although he had to confess that having the West family closing ranks around him and taking care of him had been nice.

He sat up straighter as he saw a car coming in the distance, dust rising up in its wake. As it drew closer he recognized it as belonging to Savannah Clarion.

She parked and stepped out of the car, her red hair appearing to catch fire as it sparked in the sunshine. "Hey Chase, how are you feeling?" She danced up the stairs and plopped into the chair next to him.

"Stiff and sore and maybe just a little bit cranky," he admitted.

"Men don't deal with any kind of illness well," she said. "Joshua is the worst. When he isn't feeling well he gives *cranky* a new meaning." Chase smiled. "Where's Meredith?" she asked.

"Inside. I sneaked out here to have a few minutes to myself."

"I'm going to go get her. She's going to want to hear what I have to tell you all." Savannah jumped out of the chair and disappeared into the house. A few minutes later she and Meredith came out on the porch.

"I thought you were in your room resting," Meredith said to him. "Do you need anything?"

"Yeah, I need Nurse Nancy to be off duty," he replied with a grin.

She returned his smile, obviously not offended by his words. She looked at Savannah. "So what's this news you're bursting to tell us?"

Savannah's eyes gleamed brightly. "Raymond Buchannan has been arrested and word around town is that he's at the sheriff's office with those two FBI agents, spilling his guts."

Chase wasn't surprised. From the minute Sam had told him that he'd seen Buchannan with Black, he'd known the newspaper man had something to do with the evil going on in Cotter Creek. "Have you heard who else might be involved?"

Savannah shook her head. "He was only arrested about an hour ago and so far no word is leaking out about who else might be guilty. I can't believe that man fooled me. No wonder he discouraged me from investigating the deaths in the area. He was responsible for them." Her outrage was evident in her voice.

"So it's just a matter of hours and it will all be over," Meredith said. There was something in her tone that kept Chase from looking at her, a hint of wistfulness that pierced through him and made him not want to see the expression on her face.

Just a matter of hours and it would all be over. The bad guys would be identified and arrested and Chase and Kathy's work here would be done. He'd say goodbye to the family who had embraced him and goodbye to the woman who had touched him as none ever had.

He had no other choice. As much as Meredith drew him, as much as he wanted her every minute of every day, he refused to consider anything other than telling her goodbye. He would never put anyone in the position to discover that he was his father's son. Especially not a woman he might love.

"Oh, I almost forgot." Savannah pulled an envelope out of her purse and handed it to Meredith.

"What's this?" she asked curiously.

"Beats me. It was left in the mail drop at the paper with your name on it."

Meredith opened the envelope and took out the single sheet of paper that was inside.

"What does it say?" Chase asked, although he was afraid he knew.

She looked at him, and in the shadows of her eyes he knew. "It says, 'It's time'."

Chapter 12

Meredith stared at the note in her hand. In the past four days since Chase had gotten shot she'd forgotten about the notes. Her entire focus had been Chase's health. But now the mystery of the notes and the strange, ominous feeling they brought came crashing down around her.

"It's time? Time for what?" Savannah asked curiously.

"I wish I knew," Meredith replied. "I've been getting some weird notes. I think they're from my secret admirer." She kept her voice light, as if there was nothing to be concerned about. She didn't want Savannah to know the depth of her worry.

"Maybe it means it's finally time for her secret admirer to make himself known," Chase said.

"How exciting. You'd better call me the minute you find out who it is," Savannah exclaimed. "And now I've got to get out of here. I need to get back to town in case the big news breaks."

They said their goodbyes, and Meredith watched as her friend got into her car and headed back toward town. When Savannah's car was out of sight, she sat in the chair next to Chase.

For a long moment neither of them spoke. She set the note on the floor next to her chair, not wanting to hold it in her hand another minute.

"You know, it's possible that's all it means," she finally said. She looked at him and could tell by his frown that he wasn't sure what to believe. "In any case, this is almost over for you. I guess you'll be packing up and heading back to Kansas City."

She hoped her voice didn't betray the rich emotion that filled her as she thought of him leaving. She didn't want him to know how deeply she cared, how much she'd ache when he was gone.

She'd told him she was only interested in a hot affair, no strings attached, and that's the way it had to be. Even if he wanted it otherwise, she knew that in the end she could never be what any man wanted forever in his life.

"Maybe I should hang around for a while," he said. "At least until you know the identity of this secret admirer."

"That's not necessary," she replied with forced lightness. "The more I think about it the more I think it's possible it's Buck Harmon. I think it's possible he might have even had a crush on my mother years ago. He's about the right age, and his ex-wife even looked a bit like Mom." She was rambling and wasn't sure whether she was trying to alleviate his concerns or her own.

"I still don't like the idea of leaving here and not knowing for sure if you're in any danger," he replied.

"Chase, my family members work as bodyguards. I'm probably safer than anyone else in the county." She was suddenly eager for him to go, not wanting to be around him another day, not wanting to fall any deeper in love with him than she already was.

"You haven't even told your family about the notes," he replied.

"If it will make you feel better, I will."

"When?"

She sighed. "Before you leave."

His eyes were enigmatic as he gazed at her. "We'll see what tomorrow brings," he finally said.

It was Clay who delivered the news the next morning that Raymond Buchannan had sung his heart out and named Mayor George Sharp as the brains behind the land scheme. The ambitious mayor had arranged the accidents that had occurred to the rancher and had murdered Sheila Wadsworth and who knew how many others.

They were all seated at breakfast when he came in with the story. "I always knew he was ambitious," Smokey exclaimed as if the news didn't surprise him at all.

"Apparently he was all set to be king of the condos," Clay said as he and Libby sat at the table and Gracie crawled up into Red's lap.

"Grandpa, Mr. Mayor might be king of the condos, but Daddy says Mommy is queen of the shoes," she exclaimed.

Libby laughed. "Clay doesn't understand a woman's need for more than two pairs of shoes. Tell him, Meredith, explain to him that shoes are important to a woman's mental health."

"I'm the wrong person to ask," Meredith replied. "I'm afraid I'm a dismal excuse of a woman who owns only three pairs. Sunday best, everyday and mucking boots."

Gracie crawled out of Red's lap and walked over to lean against Meredith's side. "Aunt Meredith, you come shopping with me and mommy and we'll buy you fairy-princess shoes."

Meredith laughed and gave the little girl a hug. "Don't you have to be a fairy princess to wear princess shoes?"

Gracie touched a strand of Meredith's dark hair. "You're as pretty as a fairy princess."

Meredith felt a blush sweep over her face. "And you, little one, are too sweet not to tickle." Meredith gave her tummy a tickle.

With a delighted laugh Gracie sprinted away and crawled into her mother's lap. As the conversation continued, Meredith watched Libby stroking her daughter's hair, saw the way Gracie seemed to melt into her mother with absolute trust and love.

Meredith had never thought much about having children until Gracie had joined the family. Seeing the relationship Libby had with her daughter stirred a new wistfulness in Meredith.

She'd probably never know the joys of motherhood. She glanced over at Chase, who looked better, healthier this morning than he had in the past couple of days. She'd love to have his baby, but she would never bring a child into the world without both parents being involved with each other and with the baby.

"I guess this means you'll be heading back to Kansas City," Red said to Chase. "Your work here is done." He smiled at Chase's surprised expression. "I knew you were FBI and working the case from the second day of your arrival. I'm no fool. I like to know the people who come into my house so I did a little checking."

"Does Dalton know?" Chase asked.

"All the boys know."

"Why didn't somebody say something?" Chase looked around the table.

"We respected your job and what you were trying to do," Clay replied.

Chase looked down at his plate for a long

moment, then looked at Red. "I'm sorry for the deception. It didn't sit right with me, but I had a job to do."

"No reason to apologize," Smokey replied. "I knew that woman wasn't an ordinary one the first time I saw her whip out her pistol." He smiled at Kathy. "But I don't give a damn if she's FBI or not. I still make better coleslaw than her." Everyone laughed.

It was evening when Meredith and Chase sat on the front porch watching the sun go down. "Your family humbles me," he said. "I've never felt so accepted by anyone."

A lump formed in her throat. "They know a good man when they meet one."

"I spoke with Agents Wallace and Tompkins a little while ago," he said. "They're confident that Raymond Buchannan and George Sharp were the only men in town working the deal. They also told me that Joe Black was arrested this morning at one of his properties in Aspen, Colorado. They're anticipating picking up Harold Willington in the next day or two."

"So the bad guys go to jail and all is well in Cotter Creek, Oklahoma," she replied. "When are you heading back to Kansas City?"

"I told you earlier I'm not sure I'm leaving right away," he said.

"You have to," she said, and turned in her chair to look at him. "Please, you have to leave now." His blue eyes radiated surprise as he studied her features intently. She looked away from him and stared out in the distance. "You have to go, Chase, because I can't stand it if you stick around too much longer."

Looking back at him again, she fought the wealth of emotion that pressed tightly against her chest. She got up out of the chair and walked to the porch railing so her back was to him.

"I know I told you that I was fine with just a hot physical relationship, but I didn't expect to fall in love with you. It's not your fault. You made it clear that you aren't looking for love, for commitment, and in any case I know I'm not the kind of woman men want to marry."

"What are you talking about?"

She heard him rise from his chair and felt his nearness just behind her. Tears burned at her eyes but she willed them away, refusing to allow him to see her cry.

"Meredith, what do you mean you aren't the kind of woman men marry?"

She turned to look at him, loving the lean angles of his face, the rakish scar that cut through his eyebrow and the sensual lips that were at the moment thinned and pressed tightly together. "That's what the last man I dated told me. He said I was a great girl, but when he decided to marry, it would be to a real woman, somebody soft and needy."

She shrugged. "I'm a bodyguard. I don't know much about being a woman. I only own three pairs of shoes."

"The man you were dating was obviously a fool,"

he exclaimed. "Just because you're strong and capable doesn't mean you don't know how to be a woman."

His gaze was warm and the curve of his lips were soft. "Meredith, you're sexy and incredibly feminine and more of a woman that anyone I've ever met. It would be easy for any man to fall in love with you and look forward to spending the rest of his life with you."

Her vision blurred slightly as the tears she'd tried to force back once again burned, then filled her eyes. "If what you say is true, then why didn't you fall in love with me? Why aren't you looking forward to spending the rest of your life with me?"

His eyebrows tugged together in a frown. "It's complicated."

"Yeah, right." She turned back around as tears fell onto her cheeks.

"Meredith." He grabbed her arm and forcefully turned her to face him once again. "Don't you get it? It's not about you. It's about me. Any man would be damned lucky to have you in their life. But I decided a long time ago that I wouldn't put any women at risk." He reached up and rubbed his thumb against her cheek. "Especially not you."

"At risk? What are you talking about?" She searched his features.

He dropped his hand and stepped back from her. "You know my history. You know what kind of man my father was. His blood runs inside my veins. He was my role model for too many years."

She stared at him in surprise. "And you're afraid you'll be like him?" He didn't reply, but his jaw tightened and his eyes grew darker. "When was the last time you hit somebody? When was the last time you were abusive?"

"That doesn't matter. What does matter is that I love you too much to take a chance." There was implacability in his voice.

Joy battled with despair at his words. He loved her. He loved her and he wasn't going to do anything about it. Tears once again misted her vision as despair won out. And on the heels of that despair was a hint of anger.

"You love me so much that you aren't going to reach out for happiness? You're going to turn your back on me and my love?" The anger inside her grew. "Then your father wins. He's managed to totally destroy your life."

"It's important to me that I don't destroy yours," he replied.

She needed to get away from him. The tears that she'd tried so desperately to contain needed to be released and she refused to allow them more freedom in front of him. "You lied to me, Chase. You told me that the scars your father left behind didn't even hurt anymore. But that was a lie. They must hurt like hell for you to choose to live your life alone."

She didn't wait for his reply, but instead turned and ran inside the house, needing the privacy of her room to cry, wanting the seclusion of her space to grieve for what might have been.

Sleep didn't come easily to Chase that night, and he got out of bed late the next morning with the self-loathing of a man who'd kicked a puppy in a temper fit and now regretted his actions.

But it wasn't regret that weighed heavy in his heart. He told himself that turning his back on Meredith was the right thing to do. She would eventually find another man who would love the woman she was and she would build a life with him that would banish him from her memory.

That's what he wanted for her. Happiness and love. He just knew she couldn't have that with him. Today would be his last day here. He was well enough to travel, and it was time to get out of Dodge.

Before he left he'd make sure Meredith told her family about the notes she'd been receiving and he'd get a personal assurance from each of her brothers that they would watch over her, make sure she remained safe.

He was still stunned over the fact that Kathy intended to return to Kansas City, retire, then come back out here to be with Smokey. He hadn't tried to talk her out of it when she'd told him. He'd seen the light of happiness in her eyes and knew that for the first time in her life she was following her heart.

By the time he washed and dressed, it was after ten-thirty. Breakfast had passed, but he found

Smokey and Kathy sitting at the kitchen table lingering over coffee.

"There's our lazy man," Kathy said as he walked into the kitchen.

"I can't believe I slept so late," Chase replied. He walked over to the cabinet, withdrew a cup and poured himself coffee.

"Want me to rustle you up some eggs?" Smokey asked.

"No, thanks, this will be just fine." Chase joined them at the table and took a sip of the hot strong brew.

"We were just sitting here talking about Raymond Buchannan and George Sharp," Kathy said. "I spoke with Agent Tompkins this morning and he said both men confessed to everything."

"I never trusted Mayor Sharp, but I would never have suspected that Raymond Buchannan would have been involved in anything like this," Smokey said.

"Love or money, those are the motives for most crimes," Kathy said.

"In this case love of money," Smokey replied.

"Where's Meredith?" Chase asked.

"She left about twenty minutes ago to go into town," Kathy replied.

"By herself?" Chase frowned.

Smokey released a gruff laugh. "Last time I looked she was a grown woman."

"I think she was meeting Savannah." Kathy paused and took a sip of her coffee. "She probably wants to hear all the gossip about what's happened over the past twenty-four hours."

Although there was no reason for it, Chase had a bad feeling. "I think I'll give her a quick call," he said, and excused himself from the table.

He went back to his bedroom and grabbed his cell phone, then punched in the number for hers. She answered on the second ring.

"I don't like you wandering around all on your own," he said without preamble.

"I'll be fine." Her voice held a distance that ripped through him.

"I still don't like it."

Her sigh was audible. "I'm not a fool, Chase. I don't intend to stop for anyone or anything along the side of a deserted road. I'll be around people. Believe me, I'll be fine. I'm meeting Savannah for lunch, then I'm coming back home. I should be back around two or two-thirty, long before dark."

"When you get home we need to have a talk with your family. You need to tell them about the notes before I leave here in the morning."

"No problem," she replied, then before he could say anything else she disconnected.

He closed his phone and tossed it on the bed, the feeling of disquiet growing inside him. He had a feeling he wouldn't feel good until Meredith was back at the ranch safe and sound.

Chapter 13

Meredith tossed the cell phone to the car seat next to her. She'd awakened that morning with a fierce restlessness that urged her to get out and away from the ranch, out and away from Chase.

After their conversation the night before, she'd spent the remainder of the evening in her bedroom. There was nothing more to say to him, and just the thought of looking at him had caused a stab of pain to bolt through her.

Before meeting Savannah for lunch, she intended to go to the Wild West Protective Services office and beg Dalton to find her a job, something that would take her far away from Cotter Creek, something that would take her mind off Chase McCall.

She'd told Chase the truth. She intended to be careful, to make sure she was surrounded by people throughout the day. "It's time." She clenched her fingers more tightly around the steering wheel as she thought of the note Savannah had delivered to her the night before.

"It's time." What did it mean? There was no question that the two words portended something happening. But what? Maybe after lunch she'd stop into Sheriff Ramsey's office and find out if the reports had come back from the lab on the other notes.

She told herself that surely nothing bad could happen to her on such a gorgeous autumn day. As she drove toward town she noticed how the sun dappled light through the vivid red and yellow leaves on the trees. It wouldn't be long before the leaves would fall to the ground and winter would move in with its icy grasp.

Rolling down her window she allowed the sweet scents of fall to fill the car, hoping to banish the smell of Chase that seemed to linger in her head.

He'd be gone tomorrow. Kathy had told her that morning that they planned to catch the bus back to Kansas City the next day.

She told herself she couldn't wait for him to be gone, that she was sick of his presence and tired of looking at him. But her heart knew the truth. Telling him goodbye would be the single most difficult thing she'd ever done in her life.

Pulling into a parking space in front of the Wild

West Protective Services office, she consciously willed away thoughts of Chase McCall. She had to stop thinking about him. She had to stop mourning for what might have been, for what would never be.

Dalton was behind the front desk, tossing balled-up paper into the waste-can basketball-style. "You look productive," she said dryly.

"Two points," he exclaimed as the paper hit the rim, then fell into the can. "Boredom is a terrible thing. What are you doing here?"

She sat in the chair opposite the desk. "Boredom is a terrible thing," she echoed. "I need to work. Please find me a job."

"I didn't realize you were wanting to go out. Something came in last night but I sent Joshua this morning."

"Where?"

"Oklahoma City. It's just for a day or two. Senator Abraham's son is attending a concert, and the senator wanted us to send somebody to go with him and make sure he stays out of trouble."

"Doesn't he already have bodyguards?" Meredith asked curiously.

"Yeah, but the senator wanted an outsider to keep an eye on things. Anyway, that's all I had, and now it's gone." He smiled sympathetically. "Maybe something else will come up in the next day or two."

"I hope so. If it does, I'll take it." She tried to keep the desperation out of her voice. "I never asked you, how did your date go with Melinda?"

Dalton sighed. "That woman could talk the ears off a mule and, to be perfectly honest, I found her boring. It took me months to get up my nerve to ask her out, then the date was excruciating. Thankfully she felt the same way. We agreed to be friends." He grinned at her. "It's just you and me, kid. We're the last of the Wests to find love."

She'd found it. Oh, how she'd found it, but it apparently wasn't meant to be. "As far as I'm concerned, love is vastly overrated," she replied.

"Spoken like a true cynic," he replied with a laugh. "So, what are your plans for today?"

"Lunch with Savannah."

Dalton winced. "Don't mention my name to her. She wasn't thrilled that I talked Joshua into taking the job."

"Ah, she'll be all right. She knows how important this kind of work is to Joshua." She stood and looked at her watch. "And speaking of Savannah, I'd better get out of here. I'm supposed to meet her at the café in ten minutes."

"See you later, sis." Dalton balled up another piece of paper, apparently intent on returning to his one-man trash can hoops.

Even though Savannah was rarely on time, Meredith headed for the café. She waved to Sam, who sat in his usual spot on the bench outside the barbershop, then went into the café where a lunch crowd had begun to arrive.

She found an empty booth, slid in and told the

waitress she was waiting for a friend. As she waited for Savannah she caught snippets of conversations going on at other tables. The topic of the day was definitely the arrest of Mayor Sharp and Raymond Buchannan.

She'd always hoped somewhere in the back of her mind that it would be discovered that the person or persons responsible for so many deaths would turn out to have no ties to Cotter Creek.

It was hard to digest that the men responsible had been born and raised right here and had betrayed the entire town with their evil intentions. She was glad it was over, glad that the town could now begin the healing process.

It was exactly quarter after eleven when Savannah flew through the café door and beelined to Meredith's booth. As her friend slid in across from her, Meredith saw the lines of exhaustion that rode her features.

"Remind me again of why I wanted to be a newspaper mogul," she said as she motioned to the waitress. "I was up all night getting a special edition of the paper ready."

"I hear you're single for the next couple of days," Meredith said.

"It's probably a good thing Joshua's gone because I won't have time for anything but the paper for the next two days. By the time he gets back from his assignment, the worst of the furor will be over."

Their conversation halted as the waitress arrived

to take their orders. After she left, Savannah chatted about the stress of being the new owner of the *Cotter Creek Chronicles* and the biggest news break the town had seen in years, but it was obvious she loved her new position.

"Now, tell me what's going on with you. What's wrong?" Savannah asked abruptly.

Meredith leaned back against the booth. "What makes you think anything is wrong?"

Savannah leaned forward, her gaze holding Meredith's intently. "I can see it in your eyes. Something has happened."

Unexpected tears sprang to Meredith's eyes and she hastily wiped at them. "I feel like such a fool." She stared down at the top of the table. "I made the terrible mistake of falling in love."

"With Chase." It wasn't a question but rather a statement of fact.

She looked up at Savannah. "Is it that obvious?"

Savannah smiled. "Only every minute the two of you are together. He looks at you the same way you look at him. So what's the problem?"

"The problem is he isn't in the market for a relationship with anyone. The problem is he has no desire to take things any further with me." Meredith sighed unhappily.

"Men never think they want a long-term relationship. It's up to you to convince Chase that he can't live without you."

Meredith shook her head. "You know the old

saying, 'You can lead a horse to water, but you can't make him drink.' He's leaving tomorrow to go back to Kansas City and I'll go back to my usual life."

Usual life. She wasn't even sure what that was anymore. At that moment Buck Harmon entered the café. As his gaze fell on her, he jerked his cowboy hat off his head.

He hurried over to their booth, a shy smile stretching his thin lips. "Savannah." He nodded his head with a fast bob, then turned his attention to Meredith. "You look nice today," he said. "I was sorry we didn't get to finish our dance at the Fall Festival." He worried the brim of his hat between his fingers.

"Buck, you didn't by any chance send me flowers the morning after the dance, did you?" she asked.

"No. Why? Should I have?" He looked at her in surprise.

Meredith studied his features carefully. He was over the age of forty. He obviously liked her. Although he professed not to have sent the roses, she wasn't sure if she believed him or not. "I got some flowers that morning but there was no card. I've been trying to figure out who was nice enough to send them to me."

"If they made you happy then I'm sorry it wasn't me," he replied.

At that moment the waitress arrived to deliver their orders and Buck moved away from their booth and took a stool at the counter.

"He's definitely working up his nerve to ask you out," Savannah said when the waitress had left. "But he's way too old for you. You're twenty-eight and he's on the wrong side of forty."

"I'm not exactly in the mood to go out on a date with anyone right now," Meredith replied. Was Buck Harmon just a shy man trying to get up the nerve to ask her out or was he her secret admirer?

"It's time". Never had two simple words brought with them such a feeling of quiet alarm. Never had two words evoked such a feeling of impending doom.

As she and Savannah ate lunch, she was grateful that the conversation moved away from Chase and love. Savannah talked about the challenges ahead of her in running the only newspaper in town.

"I'm going to be so involved with the daily operation that I need to hire a couple of reporters to do the actual stories. You don't have a secret burning to be a reporter, do you?" Savannah asked.

Meredith laughed. "No way. Besides, I'm not sure I'm going to stick around here for long."

"What are you talking about?"

"Savannah, I know how much you love it here, that when you came here from Scottsdale you felt as if this town was finally home for you. But it's different for me. I have a need to head to a bigger city, someplace where I won't be one of the West kids but just Meredith. I really don't expect you to understand."

Savannah drizzled ketchup across a pile of fries. "Where would you go?"

"Not far. I'd never want to be so far away that I couldn't come home pretty regularly to see everyone. Maybe Tulsa or Oklahoma City."

"Or Kansas City?" Savannah arched a copper-colored brow.

"No, not Kansas City," Meredith replied firmly. There was no way she could be in the same city as Chase and not feel his presence. There was no way she wanted serendipity to work so that she ran into him in a grocery store or at a shopping mall.

They chatted until they were finished eating, then Savannah looked at her watch and frowned. "I hate to eat and run, but I've got tons of work waiting for me at the office." She opened her purse to get out her half of the bill.

"Don't worry about it," Meredith said. "It's on me today."

Savannah paused a moment, her expression somber. "If you do move away you know I'll miss you dreadfully."

"You'll be too busy to miss me," Meredith replied with a forced lightness. "Go on, get out of here."

"Call me," Savannah said, then she whirled around and walked toward the exit.

Meredith watched as her friend left the café. If she did decide to move she would definitely miss Savannah. The two women had bonded from the first moment they'd met.

She turned her gaze toward the counter. Buck was gone. Even though he seemed like a nice enough man, she was glad he had already left. Something about him just gave her the creeps.

"It's time." How she wished she could get those two words out of her head. Tonight she'd tell her family about the notes. She knew Chase wouldn't leave unless he knew safety measures were in place for her.

She hated telling them about the notes she'd found in the shed. She knew it would reopen wounds, bring back the grief of her mother's death to them all.

She had hoped that she and Chase would be able to get to the bottom of it without involving any of her family members, but it appeared that wasn't going to happen.

After paying for the meal, she left the café and headed for the sheriff's office. She needed to find out if Ramsey had gotten any reports back from the lab about the notes she'd received. She realized it was probably a useless trip, that if he had learned anything, he would have already told them.

But she wasn't ready to return to the ranch where Chase would be. She couldn't look at him, couldn't talk to him without it hurting.

Entering the sheriff's office she was surprised to see nobody at the front desk. Usually Molly Richmond would be there taking phone calls and manning the small reception area.

Maybe she took a late lunch, Meredith thought. "Hello?" she called.

The door to Ramsey's office opened and the

sheriff looked at her in surprise. "Meredith, what are you doing here?" He motioned her in and to the chair in front of his desk.

"I came by to see if any of those lab reports had come back yet from Oklahoma City?"

Ramsey didn't take a seat behind his desk, but rather leaned against it. "Sorry to say nothing has come back. You've got to understand that those notes wouldn't be a top priority in the lab. Why? Has something else happened?"

"I got another note."

He frowned, his salt-and-pepper eyebrows drawing downward. "What did it say?"

"'It's time.' That's what it said."

"And just what in the hell is that supposed to mean?" he asked.

She shrugged. "Your guess is as good as mine."

"Did you bring the note with you?"

"No, it's at the ranch." She cursed herself for not bringing it to him. "I'll try to get back into town tomorrow and bring it to you." She stood, her business here done. "You'll let me know if you hear anything?"

"Of course," he replied.

With a murmured goodbye Meredith turned to exit the office. But before she could reach the door an electric jolt struck her from behind.

She had no time to wonder what had happened. It was like a bolt of lightning had slashed down from the sky and she was nothing more than a lightning rod.

The current sizzled through her and she immediately lost control of her arms and her legs. She felt herself falling but was unable to do anything to stop the fall. Her head banged against the floor and darkness descended.

At three o'clock Chase sat on the front porch staring down the road and looking for Meredith's car. She'd said she'd be home around two or two-thirty, and he was trying not to read anything into the fact that she was thirty minutes late.

She was having lunch with Savannah and he knew how those two loved to talk. She was probably just running late. Didn't women always run late? Besides, she was in downtown Cotter Creek in the middle of a sun-filled day. What could possibly happen to her there?

He turned as he heard the front door open and smiled at Kathy. She eased into the chair next to him, and for a moment neither of them said a word.

"You ready to leave all this?" she finally asked.

"Yeah. It's time to get back to the city," he replied.

"Are you ready to leave her?"

He didn't have to ask who Kathy was talking about. He released a long sigh. "I have to be ready."

"Are you sure you're doing the right thing? She's a fine woman."

"The finest I've ever met, but don't try to make me feel bad about the decision I've made where Meredith is concerned. I know what I'm doing and I'm doing what's best for her."

"God help every woman who has a man doing what's best for her," Kathy replied dryly.

Chase remained silent. He wasn't going to fight with Kathy about Meredith. What surprised him was that he hadn't expected to hurt while he was doing what was best for Meredith.

Before meeting her, he had thought he didn't have a heart, or at least knew that his heart was so heavily armored he hadn't worried about pain. But if there was one thing he'd learned over the past couple of weeks, it was that he did have a heart and at the moment it ached like hell. But he was determined to do the right thing, and the right thing was to walk away from Meredith.

"Regrets are a terrible thing when you get to be my age," Kathy said. "I don't regret the things I did, but I do regret the things I didn't do…like get married and have a family." She held Chase's gaze. "Don't make the same mistakes I did, Chase. Don't think that work can ever fill the hole that love should fill."

"Are you through?" he asked with more than a touch of irritation.

"I'm through."

He looked at his watch. Quarter after three. Where in the hell was Meredith? "Meredith said she'd be home around two or two-thirty," he said. "I wonder what's taking her so long?"

"If you're going to let her go, then leave her alone," Kathy exclaimed. "She was having lunch with Savannah. She's a big girl and doesn't need you to set a curfew for her. Besides, maybe she's in no hurry to come back here and spend time with you." She got up and went back inside the house.

He stared off in the distance, slowly digesting Kathy's words. Why would she want to come home and see him? He'd made it quite clear to her the night before that he intended to break her heart.

She'd told him she loved him, and there had been a moment when hope had shone from her eyes. And he'd taken that hope and crashed it to the ground. No wonder she wasn't eager to come back here and face him again.

He was probably worrying for nothing. Still, he couldn't quite shrug off the simmering concern he felt. "It's time." How he wished he knew what those words implied. Was it a threat of something bad or the promise of something good?

He knew that Meredith hadn't wanted to open a can of worms by telling her father about the notes, and yet at this very moment he realized how foolish they'd both been not to talk to Red, not to ask him about the identical notes they'd discovered in the shed.

She'd managed to lull him into keeping the secret and suddenly that felt like the wrong thing to do. With this thought in mind, he left the porch and went searching for Red.

He found him in the study, seated at the large mahogany desk. "Am I interrupting?" he asked from the doorway.

"Not at all. I'm just paying bills. A little interruption would be welcome." Red motioned him to the chair in front of the desk. "I have to admit the house is going to feel empty with you and Kathy gone."

"I have a feeling it won't be long till Kathy will be back here," Chase replied.

Red smiled. "I'm glad. Smokey has been a good friend, like a brother to me, and there's nothing I'd like to see more than him happy."

"I have something rather sensitive to discuss with you," Chase said, his mind formulating where to begin. "Meredith found some strange notes in the shed in the boxes of your wife's things."

Red frowned. "Strange notes?"

Chase nodded. "There were three of them. One said something like 'You're my destiny.' Another said 'You will be mine,' and the last one said 'It's time.' You know anything about them?"

"Not those specifically, but it wasn't unusual for Elizabeth to occasionally get those kinds of notes, especially in the first year or so that we moved out here. Some of the California paparazzi got hold of the story that she was abandoning her Hollywood dreams for love and came out here and took pictures. After they appeared in a couple of the tabloids, she got a ton of mail, both good and bad."

"So you'd have no idea when exactly she might have received those particular notes?"

"Don't have a clue. Why is it important?"

"Meredith has been getting the same notes. They

appear to be written by the same person. We think that same person sent her the roses."

Red sat up straighter in his chair and frowned thoughtfully. "I don't quite know what to make of it. Do you?"

Chase shook his head. "All I know is I don't like it."

"Why hasn't Meredith come to us about this? Why hasn't she told me or her brothers?"

"I think at first she was embarrassed. She thought it was just somebody who was too shy to approach her and she was afraid of being teased."

Red sighed. "Her brothers have always teased her unmercifully, but it's only because they care about her." He leaned back in the big, overstuffed leather desk chair and stared at a place just over Chase's shoulder. He sighed again, then directed his gaze back to Chase. "Do you think she's in danger?"

"I think it's possible," he replied.

"Where is she now?" Red asked.

"She went into town to have lunch with Savannah. She should be getting back anytime now." Chase looked at his watch. It was just after three-thirty. She wasn't so late that he should feel panicked, and yet the first stir of panic whispered in his ear.

"I was wondering if you'd mind if I borrowed your car. I thought maybe I'd take a drive into town," Chase said.

"You think she's in trouble now?" Red asked.

Chase weighed his options. He knew Red wasn't in the best of health. He also knew he had absolutely no reason to believe Meredith was in trouble except his gut instinct, and that instinct had been wrong before. "Nah, I just need to pick up a few things before Kathy and I head back to Kansas City tomorrow."

Minutes later as he drove away from the ranch he told himself he was overreacting to Meredith being late. It wasn't as if she were hours late back to the ranch. And it was possible she was intentionally staying away because she wanted to spend as little time with him as possible.

Still, all the rationalization in the world couldn't dissipate the knot of tension in his chest. He drove slowly, checking along the sides of the road for her car, grateful that he didn't see it.

As he approached the place where Elizabeth West had been found strangled to death next to her car, he hoped and prayed that the man responsible for that crime didn't now have Meredith in his sight.

It was quarter after four when he drove down Main Street and breathed a sigh of relief as he saw Meredith's car parked in front of the café.

He parked next to her car and as he got out he scanned the streets, surprised to see that Sam Rhenquist wasn't seated on the bench in front of the barbershop as he usually was. He hoped the old man wasn't sick.

Dismissing Sam from his mind, he stepped into

the café and looked around, seeking Meredith and Savannah. They were nowhere inside.

Maybe they'd gone to the newspaper office after lunch, he told himself. There was no reason to get excited just because they weren't still in the café.

He tried to quiet the whisper of panic inside him as he strode down the sidewalk toward the newspaper office. He was being ridiculous. There was absolutely no evidence that the notes were written by anyone who meant Meredith harm.

When he stepped into the newspaper office, Savannah was seated at the front desk and talking on the telephone. She held up a finger to indicate she'd be with him momentarily.

She finished the call. "Hi, Chase. Have you come to give me a tidbit of inside investigation gossip for the paper?"

"Actually, I'm looking for Meredith, but it's obvious she isn't here."

"We had lunch earlier, but we parted ways about an hour ago," Savannah replied.

"Did she mention that she had errands to run or something in particular to do? Her car is still parked in front of the café."

"She didn't mention anything, but if her car's still there then she's got to be around town somewhere," Savannah replied. At that moment the phone rang, and with a murmur of apology Savannah answered.

Chase gave her a wave, then left the newspaper office and gazed first up the street, then down.

Meredith wasn't the type of woman to spend an afternoon shopping at the few dress shops Cotter Creek had to offer.

So, where might she have gone? His gaze fell on the Curl Palace and he wondered if she might have gone in to get a hair trim. Although it seemed unlikely, he hurried down the sidewalk toward the beauty salon.

A glance inside let him know Meredith wasn't there. He stepped back out on the sidewalk, the panic that had been just a whisper before now screaming inside his head.

Chapter 14

Pain crashed through Meredith, pulling her from the darkness and into some semblance of consciousness. The back of her head felt as if it had exploded outward, and every muscle in her body hurt.

Tentatively she opened her eyes, shocked that the profound darkness didn't go away but rather lingered. It was then that she became aware of the vibration coming from beneath her and the feeling of motion.

Disoriented, she flung her hands out and tried to straighten her legs, but with a shock realized exactly where she was…in the trunk of a car.

What car? Sweet Jesus, the pain in her head made it almost impossible to think. And she had to think. She had to figure out why she was in a car trunk and how she had gotten here.

Her hand automatically went to her waist for her gun, but it was gone. She had to figure out what was happening, but it was impossible to focus on anything other than the desire not to throw up. Her head pounded and the motion of the car combined with the fumes of exhaust threatened to make her sick.

Fear added to her illness, a rich raw fear that clawed at her, that forced any thought she might have out of her head. She gave in to the fear, screaming at the top of her lungs as she kicked with all her might against the sides of the trunk.

It was only exhaustion that eventually forced her to stop. She panted to catch her breath…and remembered. She remembered lunch with Savannah. She envisioned watching Savannah leave the café. She'd remained behind and finished a cup of coffee, then had left and gone to see Sheriff Ramsey.

She'd talked to the sheriff about the notes and asked if lab reports had come back, then she'd turned to leave. And nothing. Sheriff Ramsey? Was she in the trunk of his car? But why? What on earth was going on?

Her brain began to work overtime. Sheriff Ramsey was the first person to the scene when her mother had been murdered. Or had he been there all along? Had he been the one who had strangled her, then pretended to find her car and investigate the murder?

Oh, God. Oh, God. She tried to draw deep breaths

to still the rising hysteria inside her. She was in trouble and nobody knew it. Nobody knew where she was. Nobody suspected the good sheriff was a murderer.

Where was he taking her? She had no idea how long she'd been in the truck, how long they'd been driving. She had no idea how long she'd been unconscious, how many hours had passed since she'd entered the sheriff's office.

She had to think, not about what was happening, but rather about how to get herself out of this mess. Ramsey was soft and older than her. It was possible she might be able to kick him and run if the car ever stopped. The only way she'd have a chance to escape was if he opened the trunk.

She knew the moment they left paved road and turned onto a gravel road. The gravel crunched beneath the tires, and his speed slowed. She remained lying in a fetal position, gathering her strength so she could take advantage of any opportunity for escape.

Chase. Her heart cried his name. Did he realize she was missing? She'd told him that she'd be back at the ranch around two or two-thirty. Had enough time passed that he knew she was in trouble?

She tensed as the car slowed to a mere crawl, then stopped. The engine shut off and her heart raced with terror. Rolling over on her back, she pulled her legs up, preparing to kick the first body part that came into view when he opened the trunk. Kick and run, her brain commanded. She couldn't think of Chase. She couldn't think of her mother. All she needed to focus on was kick and run.

Her heartbeat was the only thing she could hear, booming in her head. She tried to keep her breathing deep and regular as she prepared for the fight of her life.

The driver door opened, then slammed shut. She heard his heavy footsteps on the gravel as he approached the trunk. Despite the pounding of her head and the ache of every muscle in her body, she stayed focused on the trunk lid. Kick and run.

The trunk opened but before she could strike out she was hit with a stun gun. As electricity jolted through her she was helpless, a mass of uncontrollable muscles. Unable to move, she watched in horror as Sheriff Ramsey leaned over her and placed a sweet-smelling rag over her nose and mouth. Darkness crashed around her.

Consciousness returned in bits and pieces. She became aware of the fact that she was in a bed. Fresh-scented sheets covered the soft mattress beneath her, and for a moment she thought she was in her own bed, safe at the ranch.

Then she remembered. The trunk…Sheriff Ramsey. Her eyes snapped open and she found herself in a small bedroom. The walls were covered with photos and posters, and an open closet contained gowns and dresses that were vaguely familiar.

But it was the photos that held her attention.

Photos of her mother. The room wasn't a bedroom, rather it was a shrine to Elizabeth West.

She sat up and took a moment to look around, noting that the window the room boasted was boarded up and the door a jail cell door complete with steel bars.

She flung her legs over the side of the bed and stood on trembling legs. There was a doorway to her right with no door and a peek inside showed her that it was a bathroom. Everything in there was sturdy plastic and there was no mirror on the wall, nothing that could be used as a weapon or to aid her escape.

Everywhere she looked a picture of her mother returned her gaze. There were publicity shots, newspaper clippings and snapshots. In some of the snapshots it was obvious her mother hadn't known that her picture was being taken, in others she smiled into the camera with the ease of a woman accustomed to being photographed.

One photo in particular stunned Meredith. In it were three people, her mother, her father and a much younger Jim Ramsey. It had obviously been taken on a movie set. So, Jim had known her mother in Hollywood. She digested this information with a sinking horror.

It seemed obvious now that he must have followed her from California to Cotter Creek. He'd bided his time, wanting her, obsessing about her, then one night on a deserted stretch of road he'd killed her.

"Ah, I see you're awake."

She whirled around to see him standing on the other side of the steel bars. Jim Ramsey, the man who had sworn to uphold the laws of the county, the man who had murdered her mother. She said nothing.

"I'm sorry I had to be so rough with you, but things are going to be fine now." He smiled and in the light of his eyes she saw his madness. "I'm going to have to leave for a little while, but it would be nice if while I'm gone you freshened up a bit and changed into that blue dress." He pointed toward the closet area. "Remember you wore that in *Paris Nights*. That was my favorite of your movies. You were stunning in that dress."

The lines of reality had blurred for Jim Ramsey. As he stared at her, she knew he was seeing another woman in another time. "I'm not Elizabeth, I'm Meredith," she exclaimed. "Let me out of here and we'll forget all about this." It was a lie, but she needed to jar him back to reality. "Sheriff Ramsey, you need to let me go now. Elizabeth is dead and this isn't going to bring her back."

He slammed his hands against the bars, his face contorted with a sudden rage. "Shut up. You need to shut up. I've waited so long for this. You're mine. You were always supposed to be mine. I'll be back later and I want you in that blue dress."

He turned and disappeared from the doorway. A chill of horror washed over her. She was the prisoner of a man obsessed with her mother, the man she knew had killed her mother. And nobody knew where she was.

By the time five o'clock arrived, Chase knew something was terribly wrong. He first went to the sheriff's office where he was told that Ramsey was out in the field, then he went to Wild West Protective Services and told Dalton to rally the family.

Within twenty minutes Tanner, Zack, Clay and Red had joined Dalton and Chase in the office. The men wore grim expressions as Chase explained what had been going on and his concerns for Meredith's safety.

They agreed to meet back at the office in twenty minutes, then split up to check each and every store in the two-block area for signs of her.

As Chase headed for the north end of town, he tried to stop the raw emotion that threatened to consume him. He recognized it as fear, something he hadn't felt for a very long time.

He hadn't felt this kind of fear since he'd been a child and had sat in school knowing he had to go home to his father. He hadn't felt this kind of terror since the night his mother had died and he'd known that any goodness that had existed in his world had died with her. But this time his fear wasn't for himself, but rather for the woman he loved.

Even though he'd had every intention of walking away from Meredith, he wanted her alive and well when he left her. He hadn't realized how intricately his heart had wound with hers until this moment, when he sensed danger closing in around them as dark as the night falling all too quickly.

Where are you, Meredith? The evening shadows were getting darker, thicker and he had the feeling that if they didn't find her before night fell completely, they might never find her.

He raced from store to store, his heartbeat gaining speed with each step. How did a woman simply disappear? "It's time". The words echoed in his head like the notes of a dreadful song. "It's time." What in the hell did they mean?

They had all gathered back at the Wild West Protective Services office when Sheriff Ramsey walked in. As quickly as possible they told him what was going on. By that time Smokey, Kathy and Savannah had joined the search party.

"I've tried to call her cell phone a dozen times in the last hour, but she's not answering," Chase said, the sense of panic a living, breathing entity inside him.

"Is it possible she left town with somebody?" Sheriff Ramsey asked. "Maybe she met a man and they drove somewhere for dinner?"

"Not possible," Chase replied flatly. "She's in trouble and it has something to do with those notes she got."

"Maybe we should search one more time," Ramsey said. "It's possible you just missed her in one of the stores."

They agreed to spread out once again, this time

knocking on doors to the houses along Main Street to see if anyone had any information about Meredith's whereabouts.

It was only as Chase passed the barbershop and noticed once again that Sam Rhenquist wasn't in his usual place that his absence suddenly took on an ominous aura.

The man never missed a day of bench sitting, but he'd been absent from the bench the whole time Chase had been in town. He spied Dalton across the street and hurried toward him.

"You know where Rhenquist lives?" he asked.

"Sure." Dalton pointed to the barbershop. "He lives in the apartment on the second floor. Why?"

Chase didn't reply, but instead hurried across the street toward the barbershop. His gut instinct told him that Sam Rhenquist was no more a kidnapper or murderer than Chase was a Buddhist monk. He also knew he couldn't ignore an anomaly and Sam Rhenquist not seated in his usual spot was definitely an anomaly.

On the side of the building that housed the barbershop was a set of stairs that led up to the second floor. Chase took the steps two at a time, his side aching painfully and reminding him that he still wasn't up to par.

Still he didn't allow the pain to slow him. When he reached the door he pounded on it with his fist. He was vaguely aware of Dalton and Clay at the bottom of the stairs, watching with fierce intensity.

When there was no immediate reply, he pounded again, this time hearing Sam's voice. "All right, all right. I'm coming. Don't break down the damn door."

The minute he opened the door Chase realized why he hadn't been sitting on his bench. Sam looked sick as a dog. He was clad in a ratty bathrobe and looked weak as a kitten.

"Chase," he said in surprise. "Don't come any closer, boy. I've got a bug or something. I've been puking my guts up for the last couple of hours."

Chase could smell the faint scent of vomit and knew the old man was telling him the truth. "Sam, we can't find Meredith West. Have you seen her today?"

Sam frowned and clutched his robe more tightly around his thin body. "I saw her earlier. She and Savannah ate at the café, then afterward Meredith went into the sheriff's office."

Chase frowned. Ramsey hadn't said anything about seeing Meredith earlier. "Did you see her leave there?"

Sam shook his head. "It was about forty-five minutes after she went inside that I started feeling poorly and decided to come up here. Before I left the bench I didn't see her come out of the office."

What would Meredith had done in the sheriff's office for forty-five minutes? Nothing that he could think of. "Thanks, Sam."

Sheriff Ramsey? Was it possible he knew something about her disappearance? Was it possible he was responsible? A new burst of adrenaline accompanied Chase down the stairs. "Where's Ramsey?" he asked Dalton and Clay.

"I'm not sure," Dalton said. "I guess he's searching like everyone else. Why?"

"We need to find him," Chase said and strode off in the direction of the sheriff's office. Ramsey, who was first on the scene when Elizabeth West had been murdered. Ramsey, who would have helped conduct the investigation that had yielded nothing useful. Chase's head reeled with horrible suppositions.

"Chase, what's going on?" Dalton and Clay hurried to catch up with him.

Chase stopped and turned to gaze at the two men. "I think the good sheriff knows where your sister is. I also think he just might be the man who murdered your mother."

Chapter 15

"There has to be a way out," Meredith said with frustration. She'd spent every minute since Ramsey had left trying desperately to rip the boards off the window, but they were immovable. She now stood in the center of the room and looked around.

She had no idea when Ramsey might return, no idea what might happen when he did. One thing was certain, she sure as hell wasn't going to play into his fantasy by putting on one of her mother's old costumes.

There was no point in trying to get through the door. Ramsey must have plundered the city funds to buy the steel door that belonged in a prison or a jail.

She sank down on the edge of the bed and closed

her eyes, trying to figure out how she was going to get out of this mess.

She couldn't count on anyone riding to her rescue. All the time that she and Clay had discussed the murder of her mother and the notes, the sheriff would have been the last person they would have suspected.

She had the horrifying feeling that she was on her own, that if she were going to survive this it would be by being smarter and faster than the portly, crazy Jim Ramsey.

Maybe it would be smarter to play into his fantasy. Although she had no doubt in her mind that he had strangled her mother, it was also obvious that he wanted Elizabeth, needed Elizabeth. And maybe if Meredith pretended to be Elizabeth she could convince him to let her out of this cell.

She walked over to the closet where the glittery blue dress hung. *Paris Nights* had been the movie that had put Elizabeth's name on the lips of the movers and shakers of Hollywood. It had been the last movie she'd made before leaving it all behind to marry Red and move to Cotter Creek.

"Mom," she whispered as she stroked her hand down the sequin-laden fabric.

She'd never know her mother's soft touch, never have the special heart-to-heart talks that mothers and daughters shared. She'd believed that the lack of her mother in her life had somehow made her less of a woman, but Chase had taught her differently.

Closing her eyes, she remembered the desire that

had lit his eyes when he looked at her. He'd told her she was a strong and sexy woman…a *real* woman. And she believed him. Todd had been an ass, and she had been a fool to believe what he'd told her. She'd seen the truth in Chase's eyes and she embraced it into her heart, into her soul.

She pulled the dress off the hanger and laid it on the bed, then quickly pulled off her flannel shirt and jeans and pulled the dress on.

It fit as if made for her, and for a moment she felt as if her mother's arms enfolded her. The fear that had been with her since the moment she'd first regained consciousness in the trunk of the car eased.

She walked over to the wall and studied one of the photos. It was a head shot of Elizabeth. She studied each and every detail.

Her mother wore her hair parted on the left side. Meredith had always worn her hair parted down the middle. In the bathroom she found a plastic brush and comb and despite lacking a mirror, she carefully parted her hair on the left and brushed it around her shoulders.

She had a feeling if she did have a mirror she'd be stunned by her likeness to the woman who had given her birth. She knew she was playing an extremely dangerous game, but she was out of any other options.

Trembling with dread, the fear once again rising up inside her, she sat on the edge of the bed to wait for Ramsey to return.

* * *

"We can't find him anywhere," Zack announced when they were all once again gathered in the Wild West Protective Services office. "His patrol car is gone, too."

"Why would Sheriff Ramsey have anything to do with Meredith's disappearance?" Tanner asked.

"I just remembered something," Clay said. "When I was on assignment in California, Gracie's agent gave me a picture that showed Mom and Dad and Jim Ramsey."

"That's right," Red said. "Jim was a friend of ours back in Hollywood. Like me, he worked as a stunt man on lots of the movies. We all worked on several movies together." Red's face paled as his gaze met Chase's. "You think Ramsey wrote those notes to Elizabeth? You think he's the man who killed her?"

"Circumstantial evidence points that way," Chase replied. The knot in his stomach twisted so tight he had trouble catching his breath. "Anyone know where Ramsey lives?"

"He's got a little place on the west side of town. Follow me." There was fire in Smokey's eyes as he headed toward his truck. The rest of them all scrambled toward their own vehicles.

Chase and Red got into Red's car, Chase behind the steering wheel. "I helped that man get settled here in town," Red said, his vast torment evident in his voice. "He called me from California and told me he wanted to get out of the business, and I encouraged him to come here to Cotter Creek and settle in."

"Don't beat yourself up. If Ramsey wanted to be near Elizabeth you couldn't have stopped him from coming here," Chase replied.

"She would have pulled her car to the side of the road for the sheriff. Elizabeth would have felt safe stopping for him." Red released a deep sigh. "If he's hurt Meredith, I'll kill him," he said fervently. "And if I find out he is the man responsible for Elizabeth's death I'll kill him again."

Chase didn't reply, but when he thought of Meredith hurt or worse, the same killing rage filled him that he knew Red was feeling.

His hopes rose when they pulled in front of a small ranch house and the patrol car was parked out front. Lights were visible beneath the closed shades.

Everyone got out of their vehicles with the silence of thieves. "Clay, Tanner and Red, you all go around the back of the house. Zack and Smokey and I will check out the front. Kathy, call Agents Tompkins and Wallace and tell them to stand by, we might need their help." Chase kept his voice low. He didn't want Ramsey to have any warning. He pulled his gun and released the safety. "Nobody do anything until I give the word."

There was no way of knowing if Meredith was dead or alive, but he didn't want to storm the place and force Ramsey to do anything drastic.

He crept to the front window, cursing the fact that the shades were pulled tight, making it impossible to see inside. There was also no way of knowing in what room Meredith might be. He'd wanted Tompkins and Wallace here in case there was a hostage situation. Ramsey wouldn't trust his own safety to any of the West family or him, but he might trust it to FBI agents who had no ties to the town or the family.

He stepped up on the porch, careful to not make a sound, then pressed his ear against the door. *Just let me hear her voice,* he prayed. *Just let me hear her voice so I know she's all right.* But there was no sound emanating from inside the house.

The man had been sworn to serve and protect, but if what they believed were true, that oath had been twisted into something ugly, something that had allowed him to kill one woman and kidnap another.

Chase couldn't pretend to understand the forces that drove a man to commit such acts. He couldn't get into the head of a man who could kill a woman he professed to love.

Meredith. His heart screamed her name as his hand reached for the doorknob. It twisted beneath his grasp. His heart pounded like it had never done before, a racing beat that beaded sweat on his brow.

He drew a deep breath and motioned with his head for the others to move closer, then with a yell he opened the door and burst inside.

The sound of a back door splintering in its frame

accompanied him inside. With his gun leveled before him he cleared the living room. Smokey headed for the kitchen and Zack followed Chase down the hallway.

"Meredith!" Chase shouted her name as he cleared the first bedroom in the hallway.

"Kitchen clear," Clay called.

Chase ran to the next room, aware of a sticky warmth on his side. He'd reopened his wound, but he couldn't think about that now. All he could think about was Meredith and the fact that she was nowhere in the house.

"You look lovely."

Meredith shot off the bed at the sound of Jim's voice. He stood just outside the doorway, his gaze warm and loving. She wanted to throw up. Her skin crawled as if his sick gaze physically touched her.

"You told me to put on the blue dress," she said, trying to keep her revulsion from her voice. "I want to please you if I can."

He closed his eyes, as if finding her words too exquisite to believe. "I thought I'd lost you," he said, his voice soft and barely audible. He opened his eyes and stared at her with hunger. "I thought I'd lost you that night on the road. You remember, don't you?" There was a fervent light in his eyes.

"The night when I was coming home from the grocery store. The night you stopped me along the side of the road," she said.

He nodded. "I'd sent you those notes. I thought you understood. I fell in love with you the first day that I met you. We were meant to be together, but then Red stepped in and you got confused. I tried to forget you. I tried to let it be, but you haunted me. That's why I moved out here. You're why I took this job."

"But it didn't work," she said softly. "I didn't understand what you wanted, what you needed." She had no idea if she was playing this right or not, but she wanted to keep him talking on the off chance that somebody might come to help.

"I didn't blame you. I knew Red had seduced you. He'd blinded you to my love, to how happy I could make you. I was a patient man. I waited while you had all your babies. I was patient, but I knew eventually I'd get a chance to make you see that you belonged to me."

"And that chance came that night along the side of the road." She wanted to weep as she thought of her mother pulling over to meet her killer.

He nodded. "I put my lights on and you pulled right over. You looked so pretty that night." He gazed just past her, as if reliving that fateful moment in his mind. "You were wearing a skirt and a green sweater that perfectly matched your eyes. You got out of the car and asked if you'd done something wrong."

"And that's when you told me how you felt about me," Meredith said.

"I thought you'd understand, that I was your destiny, that I was the man you were supposed to be with forever, but you didn't understand." It was obvious he was getting agitated. He began to pace in front of the doorway, his hand touching the butt of his gun.

Meredith's heart jumped into her throat. Had she played the game too hard? Had she pushed him into remembering something that might cause her harm?

He stopped pacing and stared at her with accusation. "You laughed at me. You laughed and said I was being foolish, that you were Red's destiny and you would be with him through eternity. I just wanted you to shut up. I didn't want to hear it so I grabbed you and you screamed. Why did you scream?" His face grew red as he grabbed hold of the bars. "Why in the hell did you scream?"

She didn't answer, but rather remained perfectly still, afraid that by doing anything, by saying anything she'd push him over the edge.

He raked a hand through his thinning gray hair and drew a deep, audible breath. "Fate has given me a second chance. You're here with me now and I'm never going to let you go. You are my destiny."

She decided to risk it. She moved closer to the bars. "Jim, why don't you open the door so we can talk face-to-face instead of with these bars between us." If she could just get him to open the door she'd at least have a fighting chance.

A shrewd light shone from his eyes. "Do you think I'm a fool? I know it's going to take time for you to fully understand that we belong together. I have all the time in the world. Nobody will ever find us here. Eventually I'll open the door, but we have years together."

With these words he turned and left, leaving behind a cold wind of desolation blowing through her. She returned to the bed and sat, fighting a feeling of hopelessness, of helplessness.

We have years together.

She tried to imagine being here in this room for one year...two years...ten years. She'd go mad. Eventually she'd break. Somehow, someway she had to get out of here.

A deep sob welled up inside her and tears seeped down her cheeks. At that moment all hell broke loose. She jumped off the bed as it sounded as if the house was coming down.

She heard a shout. A wonderfully familiar voice. "Chase! I'm in here!" She ran to the bars and clung to them, trying to see what was happening.

A shot rang out followed by a deep silence. Her heart seemed to stop beating. Then Chase was in front of her, fumbling with a set of keys to unlock the door. As the door opened she fell into his arms, sobbing his name over and over again.

It took her a moment to realize he was crying, too. He clung to her so tightly she could scarcely breathe. "Thank God," he murmured. "Thank God you're all right."

"How did you find me?" she asked as she molded herself to him.

"It's a long story." He kissed her lips, her cheeks and her forehead, then finally released her. "Come on, let's get you the hell out of here." He took her by the hand, turned to leave and fell unconscious to the floor.

Meredith sat in the chair next to the hospital bed where Chase lay asleep. She no longer wore the blue dress but rather had on her comfortable pair of jeans and one of her flannel shirts.

It had been three hours ago that Chase and her brothers had stormed the fishing cabin where Sheriff Ramsey had taken her.

She'd gotten the story in bits and pieces on the way to the hospital, how they had frantically searched the town. How they had finally realized Ramsey might be responsible. After going to his house and not finding her there, they had checked property records and discovered that Ramsey owned the cabin forty miles outside of Cotter Creek.

Ramsey would live to spend the rest of his life in prison. It had been Red who had shot him in the leg and Chase who had tackled him to the floor, further ripping his wound in the process. After twenty-five years the mystery of her mother's murder was finally solved.

"You looked unbelievable in that blue dress, but flannel suits you better."

She leaned forward as his eyes opened and he smiled at her. "Chase." His name trembled out of her as she reached for his hand.

His smile faded and his gaze held hers intently as his fingers squeezed hers. "Did he hurt you, Meredith?"

"No, no, he didn't hurt me. He didn't touch me at all," she assured him.

He closed his eyes for a moment, relief relaxing his features. "I was so afraid we wouldn't find you." He looked at her again. "I was so afraid we'd be too late."

"He thought I was my mother. He thought he was getting a second chance to spend eternity with her. He was sick, he thought he was in love with her, but what he felt had nothing to do with love."

He closed his eyes again and was silent for so long she thought he'd fallen asleep. His hand still held hers, and the warmth of his touch wound a band of heat around her heart.

He'd saved her life. He was her hero. But more, he was the man who had made her believe in herself as a woman. He was who she wanted to spend the rest of her life with, the man she loved as she knew she'd love no other. And all too soon he was going to walk out of her life without a backward glance.

He looked at her then, as if he had picked up her thoughts out of the air. His gorgeous blue eyes stared at her for a long moment. "I thought I'd lost you. Those were the longest hours in my life, when I couldn't find you."

"I was afraid nobody would ever find me again," she said.

"For a smart man, Ramsey was stupid. That

cabin was in his name. He should have known eventually we'd find it."

"I think he had every intention of acting normal, returning each day to Cotter Creek and playing sheriff until his retirement. He never intended for any suspicion to fall on him."

"Thank God for Sam Rhenquist," Chase said. "Thank God he's as nosy as a bad neighbor and saw you go into the sheriff's office but never saw you leave."

"And thank goodness you're going to live to fight another day," she replied. She moved to pull her hand from his, finding even that simple connection too painful to endure, but he tightened his grip and held fast.

"I've been thinking. I learned about abusive love from my dad. Now I've learned about obsessive love from Ramsey. I'm thinking maybe it's time I let myself know about good, healthy love."

She stared at him wordlessly, her heart stepping up its rhythm. She wasn't sure exactly what he meant and she was so afraid of jumping to conclusions.

"You were right when you told me I'm not my father. As filled with rage as I was when we burst through the door to Ramsey's cabin, I didn't kill him. When I wrestled him to the floor to get his gun away from him, I didn't beat him to death. I don't remember ever in my life being as angry as I was then. In the important things, I'm not my father's son."

"So now that you realize that, do you intend to

do anything about it?" Her heart thundered in her chest as she waited for his reply.

He smiled then, that gorgeous sexy grin that made her want to laugh and weep at the same time. "I definitely intend to do something about it. There's this woman I'm in love with. She's bright, she's beautiful and she's more of a real woman than any I've ever met. I'm hoping she'd consider marrying me and going to Kansas City with me."

For a moment her heart was so full she couldn't speak. She finally found her voice and smiled. "I can be packed and ready to go in fifteen minutes. After all, I only have some jeans and flannel shirts and three pairs of shoes to pack."

He pulled her up from her chair then, up and into the hospital bed next to him. "You wouldn't mind leaving your family to come with me? We could visit as often as you want. I'd never want to keep you from your family."

She pressed a finger to his lips. "My mother left behind everything she knew to come here with my father. I like to think that if she hadn't been killed they would have lived out their dream, a life filled with love and passion and family. I want all that with you, Chase. I want to show you how good love can be, I want you to finally know the joy of love, real love."

He leaned forward and captured her mouth with his in a tender kiss. She was careful not to get too close to him to hurt him, aware that he was healing from the exertion that had opened up his wound again.

Still even a soft, sweet kiss from him had the ability to make her toes tingle, to flutter warmth into her heart. It was she who ended the kiss, not wanting to get anything started that they couldn't finish.

He grinned at her, that familiar sexy smile that thrilled her. "Can we talk about sex now?"

She laughed. "You have a hole in your side, you're in a hospital bed and you want to talk about sex? You're such a man, Chase."

Love poured from his eyes. "And you're quite a woman, Meredith West. My woman."

Her heart swelled with happiness, and she knew that somewhere Elizabeth West was smiling because she knew her only daughter had found the special kind of love that lasted a lifetime.

* * * * *

Mediterranean Nights

Join the guests and crew of **Alexandra's Dream**,
*the newest luxury ship to set sail on the
romantic Mediterranean, as they experience
the glamorous world of cruising.*

*A new Harlequin continuity series
begins in June 2007 with
FROM RUSSIA, WITH LOVE
by Ingrid Weaver*

*Marina Artamova books a cabin on the
luxurious cruise ship* **Alexandra's Dream**,
*when she finds out that her orphaned nephew
and his adoptive father are aboard.
She's determined to be reunited with the boy…
but the romantic ambience of the ship
and her undeniable attraction to a man
she considers her enemy are about
to interfere with her quest!*

Turn the page for a sneak preview!

Piraeus, Greece

"THERE SHE IS, Stefan. *Alexandra's Dream*." David Anderson squatted beside his new son and pointed at the dark blue hull that towered above the pier. The cruise ship was a majestic sight, twelve decks high and as long as a city block. A circle of silver and gold stars, the logo of the Liberty Cruise Line, gleamed from the swept-back smokestack. Like some legendary sea creature born for the water, the ship emanated power from every sleek curve—even at rest it held the promise of motion. "That's going to be our home for the next ten days."

The child beside him remained silent, his cheeks

working in and out as he sucked furiously on his thumb. Hair so blond it appeared white ruffled against his forehead in the harbor breeze. The baby-sweet scent unique to the very young mingled with the tang of the sea.

"Ship," David said. "Uh, *parakhod*."

From beneath his bangs, Stefan looked at the *Alexandra's Dream*. Although he didn't release his thumb, the corners of his mouth tightened with the beginning of a smile.

David grinned. That was Stefan's first smile this afternoon, one of only two since they had left the orphanage yesterday. It was probably because of the boat—according to the orphanage staff, the boy loved boats, which was the main reason David had decided to book this cruise. Then again, there was a strong possibility the smile could have been a reaction to David's attempt at pocket-dictionary Russian. Whatever the cause, it was a good start.

The liaison from the adoption agency had claimed that Stefan had been taught some English, but David had yet to see evidence of it. David continued to speak, positive his son would understand his tone even if he couldn't grasp the words. "This is her maiden voyage. Her first trip, just like this is our first trip, and that makes it special." He motioned toward the stage that had been set up on the pier beneath the ship's bow. "That's why everyone's celebrating."

The ship's official christening ceremony had

been held the day before and had been a closed affair, with only the cruise-line executives and VIP guests invited, but the stage hadn't yet been disassembled. Banners bearing the blue and white of the Greek flag of the ship's owner, as well as the Liberty circle of stars logo, draped the edges of the platform. In the center, a group of musicians and a dance troupe dressed in traditional white folk costumes performed for the benefit of the *Alexandra's Dream*'s first passengers. Their audience was in a festive mood, snapping their fingers in time to the music while the dancers twirled and wove through their steps.

David bobbed his head to the rhythm of the mandolins. They were playing a folk tune that seemed vaguely familiar, possibly from a movie he'd seen. He hummed a few notes. "Catchy melody, isn't it?"

Stefan turned his gaze on David. His eyes were a striking shade of blue, as cool and pale as a winter horizon and far too solemn for a child not yet five. Still, the smile that hovered at the corners of his mouth persisted. He moved his head with the music, mirroring David's motion.

David gave a silent cheer at the interaction. Hopefully, this cruise would provide countless opportunities for more. "Hey, good for you," he said. "Do you like the music?"

The child's eyes sparked. He withdrew his thumb with a pop. *"Moozika!"*

"Music. Right!" David held out his hand. "Come on, let's go closer so we can watch the dancers."

Stefan grasped David's hand quickly, as if he feared it would be withdrawn. In an instant his budding smile was replaced by a look close to panic.

Did he remember the car accident that had killed his parents? It would be a mercy if he didn't. As far as David knew, Stefan had never spoken of it to anyone. Whatever he had seen had made him run so far from the crash that the police hadn't found him until the next day. The event had traumatized him to the extent that he hadn't uttered a word until his fifth week at the orphanage. Even now he seldom talked.

David sat back on his heels and brushed the hair from Stefan's forehead. That solemn, too-old gaze locked with his, and for an instant, David felt as if he looked back in time at an image of himself thirty years ago.

He didn't need to speak the same language to understand exactly how this boy felt. He knew what it meant to be alone and powerless among strangers, trying to be brave and tough but wishing with every fiber of his being for a place to belong, to be safe, and most of all for someone to love him….

He knew in his heart he would be a good parent to Stefan. It was why he had never considered halting the adoption process after Ellie had left him. He hadn't balked when he'd learned of the recent claim by Stefan's spinster aunt, either; the absentee relative had shown up too late for her case to be considered. The adoption was meant to be. He and this child already shared a bond that went deeper than paperwork or legalities.

A seagull screeched overhead, making Stefan start and press closer to David.

"That's my boy," David murmured. He swallowed hard, struck by the simple truth of what he had just said.

That's my *boy.*

"I can't be patient, Rudolph. I'm not going to stand by and watch my nephew get ripped from his country and his roots to live on the other side of the world."

Rudolph hissed out a slow breath. "Marina, I don't like the sound of that. What are you planning?"

"I'm going to talk some sense into this American kidnapper."

"No. Absolutely not. No offence, but diplomacy is not your strong suit."

"Diplomacy be damned. Their ship's due to sail at five o'clock."

"Then you wouldn't have an opportunity to speak with him even if his lawyer agreed to a meeting."

"I'll have ten days of opportunities, Rudolph, since I plan to be on board that ship."

* * * * *

*Follow Marina and David as they join
forces to uncover the reason behind
little Stefan's unusual silence, and the
secret behind the death of his parents....*

*Look for FROM RUSSIA, WITH LOVE
by Ingrid Weaver
in stores June 2007.*

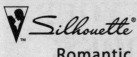

Silhouette®

Romantic
SUSPENSE

Sparked by **Danger,**
Fueled by **Passion.**

*This month and every month look for
four new heart-racing romances
set against a backdrop of suspense!*

Available in June 2007

Shelter from the Storm
by **RaeAnne Thayne**

A Little Bit Guilty
(Midnight Secrets miniseries)
by **Jenna Mills**

Mob Mistress
by **Sheri WhiteFeather**

A Serial Affair
by **Natalie Dunbar**

Available wherever you buy books!

Visit Silhouette Books at www.eHarlequin.com   SRS0507

REQUEST YOUR FREE BOOKS!

2 FREE NOVELS PLUS 2 FREE GIFTS!

Silhouette® Romantic

SUSPENSE

Sparked by Danger, Fueled by Passion!

SRS07

HARLEQUIN®
Super Romance®

Acclaimed author
Brenda Novak
returns to Dundee, Idaho, with

COULDA BEEN A COWBOY

After gaining custody of his infant son,
professional athlete Tyson Garnier hopes to escape
the media and find some privacy in Dundee, Idaho.
He also finds Dakota Brown. But is she ready for the
potential drama that comes with him?

Also watch for:

BLAME IT ON THE DOG by Amy Frazier
(Singles…with Kids)

HIS PERFECT WOMAN by Kay Stockham

DAD FOR LIFE by Helen Brenna
(A Little Secret)

MR. IRRESISTIBLE by Karina Bliss

WANTED MAN by Ellen K. Hartman

Available June 2007 wherever Harlequin books are sold!

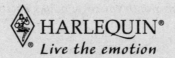

HARLEQUIN®
Live the emotion

COMING NEXT MONTH

#1467 SHELTER FROM THE STORM—RaeAnne Thayne
He was responsible for her father's downfall and must now work with
the woman he's long desired to save a young girl from a vicious crime
ring. As they move forward with the case, his secret could endanger their
victim—and his heart.

#1468 A LITTLE BIT GUILTY—Jenna Mills
Midnight Secrets
Their attraction has been building since the moment they were assigned to
capture a murderer. But when he discovers that she's been hiding a secret
agenda that threatens his career, he must decide what's more important:
exploring a potential love interest…or revenge.

#1469 MOB MISTRESS—Sheri WhiteFeather
When a Texas-bred cowboy discovers he's the prized grandson of an
infamous mob boss, he must come to terms with his new identity while
resisting the allure of the mysterious woman claiming to know the dark
secrets of his past.

#1470 A SERIAL AFFAIR—Natalie Dunbar
Special Agent Marina Santos gets an unexpected surprise when she's
assigned to work with her ex-love, Lt. Reed Crawford. Neither is happy
to see the other, but both must overcome their grudges to catch a serial
killer…even if it rekindles a spark they weren't prepared for.

SRSCNM0507